IT'S JUST ME AND YOU 2

Ah'Million

Lock Down Publications and Ca$h Presents

It's Just Me and You 2

A Novel by *Ah'Million*

Ah'Million

Lock Down Publications
Po Box 944
Stockbridge, Ga 30281

Visit our website @
www.lockdownpublications.com

Copyright 2023 by Ah"Million
It's Just Me and You 2

Lock Down Publications
Like our page on Facebook: Lock Down Publications @
www.facebook.com/lockdownpublications.ldp
Book interior design by: **Shawn Walker**
Edited by: **Sunny Giovanni**

Stay Connected with Us!

Text **LOCKDOWN** to 22828 to stay up-to-date with new releases, sneak peaks, contests and more…
Thank you.

Submission Guideline.

Submit the first three chapters of your completed manuscript to ldpsubmissions@gmail.com, subject line: Your book's title. The manuscript must be in a .doc file and sent as an attachment. Document should be in Times New Roman, double spaced and in size 12 font. Also, provide your synopsis and full contact information. If sending multiple submissions, they must each be in a separate email.

Have a story but no way to send it electronically? You can still submit to LDP/Ca$h Presents. Send in the first three chapters, written or typed, of your completed manuscript to:

LDP: Submissions Dept
Po Box 944
Stockbridge, Ga 30281

DO NOT send original manuscript. Must be a duplicate.

Provide your synopsis and a cover letter containing your full contact information.

Thanks for considering LDP and Ca$h Presents.

ACKNOWLEDGEMENTS

All glory goes to God for giving me breath and discipline to keep going. Some days are harder than most, but you can't let your circumstances dictate your amount of effort. All the women on HB... I know I made it out, but I'm sending love until this pen runs out of ink. Keep waking up and going to sleep. They can't hold you forever. Utilize the time productively so that your plans flourish exceptionally. Jazz, Sakey, B. Giles, Christina, gang gang...it's free y'all, until y'all are free. The only way is up from here. As for my Queens, don't focus on what it could be. _Pay attention to what it is. Don't let nothing come in between you and your peace. It's more precious than gold...

Continue to show support as I show my appreciation in return. Derrick, Kenny, Ma, and Pops, I love you. Del D, just know things will get better soon. I love you.

Ah'Million

Previously on: *It's Just Me and You Part 1*

Myesha

Myesha sat in the passenger seat of her sister's car. Brandi was inside of the beauty supply house picking up a few items.

Ring! Ring!

Myesha snapped her head in the direction of the ringing phone that sat in the cup holder.

"Mama." Myesha declined the call, then deleted it from Brandi's call history.

"My bad, girl. I almost had to curse that damn Chink out," Brandi rambled, climbing inside the car. "So have you thought about it?" she asked, pulling away from the store.

"Yes, and I'm not going." Myesha paused.

"I don't think Dooski believes I was with Jewel that night. He gives me this ol' suspect-ass look every time it comes up."

Brandi waved her hand. "Girl, that ain't shit. It's gon' be a whole lot of money in that motherfucka," Brandi chanted.

"More money than last time?" She had made close to five Gs. Now that she had a taste of fast money, she was hooked.

Brandi slowly nodded her head. A mischievous smile decorated her face.

"Count me in."

"Hell yeah, let's go fuck up some commas."

"Brandi." Myesha paused.

"'Sup?"

"Have you talked to Mama?"

Brandi looked at Myesha like she had two heads. "Hell nah! I don't even have her number saved in my phone. I don't fuck with her.

"Okay." Myesha nodded slowly, confused as to why her sister would bluntly lie to her.

"Why do you ask that?

"Well, I asked 'cause——"

Ring! Ring! Ring!

"Hold on," Myesha said, getting her phone out of her purse. It was Dooski. "Hey baby," she answered coolly.

"Bae, some niggas just shot up Blotchy's car! Jewel was in there! We up here at Baylor. Hurry up!"

CHAPTER 1
Myesha

"Fuck!" Myesha punched the dashboard repeatedly. "FUCK! FUCK! FUCK!" she continued. "Take me to Baylor right now! Hurry up!" Her hands trembled and tears filled her bedroom eyes.

Brandi pulled out of the parking space and off the lot. "Myesha, calm down!" she yelled. Fear coupled with shock, and Brandi drove like she was being chased. Whatever it was, it was serious.

Tears spilled from her eyes down her cheeks. "It's all my fault!" She wiped the snot as it fell.

Brandi's eyes squinted in confusion. "How is what your fault? We've been together damn near all day."

With both hands, she palmed her face and sobbed like a new-born.

Instead of bombarding her with more questions, Brandi stayed silent, assuming whatever was going on, she'd talk about it whenever she was done crying about it.

"How far away are we?" Myesha asked ten minutes later. Her face was soiled.

"According to my GPS, we'll be there in twenty-six minutes." Brandi's heart raced in anticipation. She was anxious to know what was going on.

I have to tell Bobby. Instead of calling, Myesha shot him a text instead. "Jewel is at Baylor."

Brandi gasped sharply. "What for?" she asked, gripping the steering wheel tighter.

"Jewel was in the car with her dude when someone shot the car up." Myesha squeezed her eyes shut as she spoke to prevent the tears from falling. Jewel meant everything to her. She wasn't her blood sister, but she'd choose Jewel over Brandi and Bianca any day.

"Oh my God," Brandi whispered, appalled.

"Just hang tight, we're almost there."

***

BOBBY

"Oooh, Bobby, I love this dick," Kesha cooed. She lay on top of the sheet spreadeagle.

Bobby jabbed her box as if it was the opponent. It was merely round two, and Kesha was worn out. She didn't even have the strength to lift on her elbows. All she could do was lay there and take the wood. He was serving her every inch of it. Angry and disappointed, Bobby had been taking his frustrations out on Kesha for almost an hour.

"Bae, I'm cummin'."

Bobby gritted his teeth at the sound of her voice. He had managed to paint a mental picture of Jewel, bringing him to a well-needed bust. However, the moment "bae" fell from her lips, he was snapped back into reality. Jewel called him zaddy. He wished it was her underneath him instead of Kesha.

Kesha's body jerked uncontrollably. Her warmth oozed onto Bobby's pole, leaving him no choice.

"Mmmmph," he murmured forcefully. He gave one final deep thrust, then eased out and onto his back. Bobby had been stressed since his little run-in with Sierra. Jewel's bullshit on top of that did not make things any easier.

He grabbed the soaked and saggy condom as he made his way to the restroom. Assuming her juices soaked the condom and that was the reason behind his moist hand, he eased it off and held it up. Nut gushed out of the opening on the side. *Motherfucker busted! Shit!*

"Kesha!" He hovered over her.

"Huh?" She jumped up in shock. She peered at him and then around the room. "What? What's going on?"

"The condom busted. Make sure you go get a plan B." He opened his dresser and removed a hundred dollar bill from the wad of money, tossing it on the bed before retreating back to the restroom.

Bobby hopped in the shower. He had a lot to do today and lay-ing around wasn't one of them. His mind was made up. He was go-ing to tell Kad and face whatever consequences that awaited. Some-one holding something so meaningful over his head reminded him of his prison days. On the inside, he was a loner and never asked for nothing he didn't have. He would just rather go without. He des-pised the feeling.

Bobby walked into his bedroom in pursuit of his phone. He looked on the night stand. It wasn't where he left it. *The fuck?* "Let me see your phone."

Slowly, Kesha reached under the pillow and handed Bobby her phone.

He sighed deeply upon hearing his voicemail. She had done it again. "Bruh, what did I tell you 'bout cutting my damn phone off?"

Kesha slid out of bed. Her caramel complexion complemented her flawless skin and curvaceous physique. Her walk could attract a crowd of racists and her smile was more contagious than COVID, the Omnicron strand. She squatted beside the bed, pulling the long strands of platinum blonde hair behind her ears. She eased onto her knees, her ass tooted in the air as she reached under the bed. She lifted up with Bobby's phone in hand and handed it to him. His glare imparted so much hate that it scared Kesha. She jumped back into bed.

"Uh-uh, you might as well get dressed, 'cause I'm about to head out."

She smacked her lips and continued to lay there. Unbeknownst to Bobby, she was crying silent tears. Kesha was drained with Bobby's nonchalance. She had been giving 110% for years and only getting thirty percent in return. It was time she walked away - if only her feet would allow her.

"What the fuck!"

Kesha tensed up at the sound of Bobby's outburst.

"Myesha, what's going on?" His eyes bucked in anger, but fear didn't trail too far behind. Bobby disconnected the call and hopped to his feet. "Bruh, didn't I tell you to put your shit on a long time ago?"

She swiped away the evidence where she had been crying. "Come on!"

She hopped up without putting on any underclothes, just her leggings and crop top, and grabbed her belongings.

Bobby's heart raced the closer he got to Jewel. Usually he would've taken Kesha back home, but the child in him let her tag along. A part of him wanted Jewel to feel exactly how he felt when she arrived at his place in the wee hours of the morning. He knew she had been with another man.

He hopped out of his Escalade, pulling up his Amiri jeans. He darted around the crowd of people and toward the entry. He could hear Kesha trailing closely behind him. Inside, he rushed to the desk.

A middle-aged Hispanic woman sat behind the desk. She jumped in fear at his sudden presence.

"My gir——" He paused. "I mean, my niece was shot."

"What's her——"

"Bobby!" It was Myesha and another chick.

"What happened? What's going on?" He peered over Myesha's shoulder at Dooski. His lip curled upward. Bobby's mug was vicious. He didn't know dude, but he had seen him before. Even though there wasn't no beef, there was something that Bobby simply had against men. If he didn't fuck with you, he didn't like you. Period. He could've been the guy Jewel was with the other night, for all he knew.

"I don't know." She wiped her eyes. "I was with Brandi at the store and my baby called me and told me Blotchy's car had been shot up and Jewel was in the car with him," she explained, pointing back at Dooski.

Bobby scowled, his face scrunched tightly. Dumbfounded was an understatement. He slid his phone down into the pocket of his jeans, then pulled them up. "Wait, what?" Bobby shrieked.

The doctor cleared his throat, announcing his presence. "Excuse me, are you guys here for Ms. Jewel McVale?"

"Yes," everyone voiced except Bobby. He was furious. *What the fuck was she doing with this hoe-ass nigga?* He needed answers.

"Calm down. Everything is fine. She does need a blood transfusion due to the massive loss of blood, so she will stay overnight. The bullet grazed her shoulder. She's lucky. You can go see her now."

Everyone took off in the direction of her room. Bobby and Kesha trailed close behind Myesha, since neither of them knew where the room was located.

"What about Blotchy?" Dooski asked, a bit frustrated.

Bobby slowed up at the mentioning of Blotchy's name. However, he was still carefully watching which room Myesha went in.

"After he's properly bandaged, he'll be released today. He was hit, however, the bullet went straight through without contacting any bones or arteries."

Bobby turned his mouth downward and nodded silently as they headed into Jewel's room.

JEWEL

Jewel's eyes fluttered open. Myesha hovered over her, caressing her face.

"Hey girl," Jewel said in a whisper-like tone. She smiled weakly at her cousin, pretending to be strong.

"You okay?" Myesha asked, tears falling onto Jewel's bed.

Jewel sat up a bit. "I'm fine. I'm glad it only grazed me." She winced. "I can imagine how much pain I'd be in if it would've gone in."

Bobby entered, then Kesha. Jewel licked her chapped lips. Her brows dipped in confusion as she peered at Bobby, then the woman. *She's beautiful. I know her.*

"You good?" he asked, standing beside Myesha, yet he was so close she could feel his breath. He was upset. She could see the muscle in his jaws flexing, something she noticed whenever he was angry.

"You gon' tell ya pops, or I'm gon' tell him."

"It's only going to stress him out. I'm okay."

The sound of the door grabbed all of their attention. Blotchy and Dooski rushed in. Blotchy clutched his neatly-wrapped arm. Ignoring Bobby's presence, he rushed to the opposite side of Jewel's bed.

"I'm sorry, bae, I would've never intentionally put your life in danger."

"Yeah, but you did. You don't have no business around her anyways." Bobby glared at Blotchy, walking toward him.

"Blotchy?" Kesha asked, appearing dumbfounded.

"Kesha?" He returned the same look.

Bobby paused.

"Bobby, this is my little cousin Blotchy. Blotchy, this Bobby," she introduced, secretly trying to kill the tension.

"This ain't no meet and greet. I know this fuckboy!" Bobby leaned in.

"Chill, bruh," Dooski intervened, blocking Bobby's path.

"You can get yo' one next, but I want him first."

"Run that shit! Bruh I'ma bang, and that's on gang!" Blotchy yelled. Blotchy pulled his jeans up with his good arm,

"He hurt though. There's always next time," Dooski spat. The glare in his eyes spoke louder than his words.

Bobby pulled up his jeans. "I'll catch 'em next time, but since you look like you want to buck, let's catch ours right now," Bobby voiced, ready for whatever.

"Uh-uh, hell nah. Y'all not about to do this!" Myesha stood in between them. She turned and faced Dooski, using all her might and strength to push him back.

The door opened, stealing all of their attention

"Excuse me, ladies and gentlemen." The detective paused. "Could you give me a few minutes? I need to ask her a few questions.

"She don't speak pig Latin," Blotchy voiced.

"Excuse me?" The Caucasian detective peered in his direction.

Blotchy mugged the detective and headed towards the door. He looked over his shoulder at Jewel, and the menacing look disclosed so much malice it sent shivers down her spine. *What's that about?*

She was clueless to what was occurring and all the events that led up to this point. Bobby walked past her without even looking in her direction.

"Bobby." She paused. "Ms. Taylor." Jewel mentioned to his grandma.

He stopped and sighed deeply before proceeding out.

"Hey, I know we were not the best of friends, but I hope you feel better so you can return to school," Kesha voiced, then flew after Bobby.

That's right. The night school. Jewel's faint smile was counterfeit as a three dollar bill. It was fitter for her to smile then speak. Speaking would've simply complicated things. She was in no shape for that at the time. *She must be the reason why he treats me like a prostitute.* Tears brimmed her eyes as she watched the both of them leave. *What does she have that I don't?*

Ah'Million

CHAPTER 2

KAD

"Play it again," Kad said.

Bobby played the recording for him. Kad massaged his chin while clenching his teeth. He knew who it was after hearing the recording the first time. Hearing it again simply confirmed his speculation. He shook his head slowly in disbelief. The recording stopped.

"You know who it is, fam?" Bobby asked.

"Yeah. One of 'em is that Saltine I was fucking." Kad paused. "I don't know who the other one is."

"Damn, I listened to that shit a hundred times and couldn't even tell that was Susie's ass," Bobby admitted. He could've recognized the voice if he spent more time at the office. Bobby allowed Kad to micromanage everything in regards to the organization and if he needed his assistance, he was there .Other than that, he was in the streets or in the studio.

"Bobby, I need a favor."

Bobby tensed up. The last time Kad mentioned something to this extent, it cost him ten years in prison.

"Look, I already know what you think. It's not like that," Kad spoke up quickly. Bobby had made it plain and clear when he was released years ago that he wouldn't allow someone else to jeopardize his freedom again.

"I'm listening."

"I need you to snatch Susie up. Get her on your team. Make her fall in love with you."

Agreeing to this meant hurting Jewel. Bobby tightened his jaws. "I can do that," he responded with a bite.

"If you can just get her to admit her bullshit, that's my ticket up out of here."

"Bet."

They talked about work and music before the call ended.

Kad sighed deeply, then hung up the phone. He looked around the day room. He was tired of being there. Tired of the same routine. Tired of seeing niggas.

"Kad, what's up, boy? Be my partner while Tonk at his visit!" Zip hollered from the other end of the day room. Zip was an older dude. He was wiser than most, yet very down to earth. He simply had an obsession with selling drugs. This time would make it his fifth time down for possession and manufacturing with delivering.

Kad walked over, scratching his head before sitting down. He really didn't want to play, but there was no use in wallowing in his own misery.

Zip took a sip from his cup. "Ahhh," he sounded. He licked his lips before placing the cup back on the table.

This nigga act like he really drinking something.

"Fideen!" Vic shouted, slamming the domino against the stainless steel table.

"Tia and Tamera!" Zip shot back.

"Every time you call some money, just know I'm getting mine too," he continued, slamming another domino. Kad peeped the lax look in Zip's eyes. Zip took another sip. "What's in that cup, skool?" Kad scowled curiously.

"Lean."

Kad turned his lips upward in disbelief.

"I'm for real!" Zip said, passing Kad the cup.

Without questioning, he took a sip. Secretly, Kad had become a codeine fiend since the death of his longtime girlfriend and baby mother Danielle.

Zip smirked. "Go on, you can have that. I got some more. Keep sipping, youngsta."

CHAPTER 3
KESHA

Smoke filled Kesha's black Camry as she rocked slowly back and forth in her seat. She had been parked in the lot of the hospital for almost an hour, contemplating her next move.

Tap! Tap! Tap!

She jumped at the sound before peering up into the eye of her close friend, Monica. Kesha waved her to the other side. She needed her girl to hear her out.

"What's the emergency?" Monica hopped in, slamming the door shut. The wintry night quickened her pace.

"Bobby's fucking her, Monica. I can feel it." Tears filled her eyes before spilling down her cheeks.

"Are you sure, Kesha?" Monica could hear the pain Kesha felt simply by her tone of voice, yet she wanted something concrete instead of Kesha's gut instinct. "Did they say anything?"

Kesha wiped her face clean with her hands. "No, they didn't! But I'm a woman, Monica." Kesha softly patted her chest. "I know my man. It was the way he looked. The unrelenting hate he felt towards her guy." Kesha closed her eyes and shook her head. She opened her eyes and turned to face Monica. "I know you are probably scared and don't want any parts of this, but mark my words."

"What exactly do you want me to do?" Kesha had proven her loyalty on many occasions. Monica felt obligated to complete the task her friend had set out for her. She just hated that this was the task that had fallen into her lap.

"Get rid of the bitch!" Kesha spat.

Monica rolled her eyes. "Now how would that look?" A woman dies from a bullet that grazed her. They'll be on my ass and whoever else entered her room."

Kesha smacked her lips. "Fuck it. I'll do it." Kesha tightened her jaws then unloosened her seat belt. She was determined. Every time she would think she had Bobby's undivided attention, someone or something would arise and completely distract him, sending her tumbling down to last place.

Creases formed in Monica's forehead as she peered at Kesha in disbelief. "Are you serious?"

"Serious as you were when you had me finessing and sexing your dude's victim so he won't protest against his parole." Kesha rolled her eyes.

Monica lowered her head and sighed deeply. "You right," she said in a whispery tone.

"I know I am. You did what you had to do for your piece of dick. I'm surely gon' do what I have to do for mines."

"Let's plan." Monica cut her eyes at Kesha, then flickered the tip of her nose.

***

Kesha waddled into the hospital. Jewel's room number was permanently etched inside her mental. She had one mission and one mission only. Since Kesha was an intern at the same exact hospital during the weekdays, she had to definitely be incognito. It was a good thing masks were still mandatory in hospitals. Appearing to be a distressed pregnant woman, she leaned into the counter breathlessly. Luckily, her intern hours were six a.m. to one p.m. Therefore, she had never seen or spoken to the receptionist in front of her.

"Are you okay, ma'am?"

"I'm fine. I'm just having trouble breathing," she lied.

"Are you having contractions?"

"No, not all." Kesha sighed deeply. "I'm not due or anything of that nature. I'm just six months," she added.

"Okay, have a seat over there." She pointed. "Someone will be with you shortly."

Unbeknownst to the onlookers and the receptionist, the only thing Kesha carried in her stomach were clothes. The oversized hoodie concealed the lumps from the clothes, making her stomach appear round as a ball. It wasn't even five minutes before a couple and a toddler entered.

Kesha looked left to right to ensure no one was watching her. Everyone else in the lobby was truly seeking medical attention.

Kesha was the furthest thing from their mind. Seeing the reception-ist occupied, she calmly stood and waddled to the restrooms. She knew the hospital front and back. Leaving the ER for the other side wouldn't be a problem. She darted inside the stall and undressed, changing into her scrubs. She folded the clothes she had on neatly and tightly, then pushed them under the commode. The wig and heavy foundation made Kesha look ten years her senior. The few shades darker foundation also changed the color of her complexion. She pushed the small round glasses back onto her nose. The paper-work in her hand was nothing but a stack of copies of an upcoming volleyball event that she found on top of the mailboxes inside of her apartment complex. She even tried disguising her walk as she headed to Jewel's room. She kept her head low, pretending to be reading the paperwork as she peered over the rim of her glasses. Her heartbeat thunderously in her chest the closer she got.

This is it.

She inched closer, placing her hand on the knob. She turned it slowly then opened it. Kesha's eyes widened at the sight of Bobby.

What is he doing here?

His back was to her, but he was facing Jewel. She was about to turn around and walk out, but Bobby's words ceased her movement and breathing all at once.

"So I had to find out under these circumstances that you're pregnant? Really, bruh?"

"I swear, Bobby, I just found out myself."

Kesha's chest rose and fell as hot tears streaked her cheeks. She swiftly wiped her tears away with one hand.

"That's why I had to stay overnight for the blood transfusion."

"So whose is it?"

"What?" Jewel shot back.

"Don't act appalled. It's something going on. He calling you bae and shit." Jewel lowered her head. "Is it mine or that nigga's?" Bobby spoke through clenched teeth, barely audible.

However, Kesha had picked up everything. Sweat beads formed across Kesha's forehead as she tried silently to control her breath-ing. The room seemed to have gotten smaller as she began to panic.

She cleared her throat. Bobby's and Jewel's heads swiveled in her direction. "Excuse me, sir, there is no visitation at th-this time."

"Yes ma'am, I'm leaving. No one made me leave, so I stayed," he lied, grabbing his coat off the arm of the chair. Although he didn't sneak in, he paid his way inside of the hospital and into Jewel's room.

Kesha's hands shook uncontrollably. It wasn't long before those stacks of papers went crashing into the tile floor. Bobby quickly rushed to her aid. Kesha moved as swiftly as her arms would allow. She had managed to gather them all but one.

He picked it up. "Here you—"

Kesha reached to snatch the paper out of his hand, but it didn't budge. He peered down at the paper, then back up at her, confusion etched deeper than an old scar.

Shit, he knows it's me. Kesha dropped her head. "I have to go check on the next patient." She hurried out of the door, leaving him standing there speechless.

CHAPTER 4
MYESHA

"Alright, I'm about to get outta here. I have to head to ATL in the morning."

Dooski and Blotchy slapped hands and hugged briefly.

"Bet. You sure you don't want me to go with you?" Dooski offered, peering down at the cast on Blotchy's arm.

"Yeah, baby, I'm good. Chill and enjoy, bae." He turned around and headed for the door, locking eyes with Myesha along the way. He smiled at her mischievously. Sarcasm dripped off him profusely. She smiled and looked away, afraid Dooski would read her like a book and decipher the truth.

She locked the door behind Blotchy and ran after him. Dooski lay on top of the sheets listening to the instrumental blaring from the laptop. Myesha removed her flip flops and climbed in bed next to him. With one arm wrapped around Myesha, he continued to softly pat his chest to the beat. He mumbled something Myesha couldn't understand, yet she bobbed her head to the beat anyways. There was no denying his love for music. He listened to instrumentals more than anything. She just never heard anything other than mumbling.

"Bae, let me hear you spit something." She batted her eyelashes and snuggled closer. The corner of his mouth curled upward. "I'm serious!" Myesha playfully hit him. Dooski smacked his lips. "For real, bae, just something off the dome. Let me pick the instrumental." She grabbed the laptop and sat up in bed.

He chuckled and peered around the room as soon as the Beat King instrumental blared through the laptop. He rubbed the hairs on his chin and nodded his head. "Off the dome?" he asked, peering at her.

Myesha smiled and nodded her head.

"Draco make 'em dirty dance
.38 in my pants. Just popped a few Xans
Booty put me in a trance. Uh-huh, yeah.
Pussy prettier than a lotus

Spell on me, no potion.
She rub it in like its lotion.
Now it got ha' skin glowin', aye
Designer on, she lit
Hair long and she thick
Knocked her down at the Ritz
Beat it up, Earl Spence…"

"Aye!" Myesha jumped on top of him.

Dooski chuckled, wrapping his arms around her small frame. "You like that?" he asked.

"Man, bae, that's a club banga," she responded in excitement. "Was you talking about me?" she asked, peering up at him.

Dooski chuckled softly, exposing his deep dimples. "Of course I was, bae." He leaned in and pecked her juicy lips. "You know you got that good-good."

"Bae, why you didn't try to get a deal with my uncle and Bobby? If you did that off the dome, I can only imagine what you have written."

Dooski sighed deeply. He had asked Blotchy more than once to put him on with Kad's label.

"I asked that nigga, but——"

Myesha cut him off, holding her hand up to cease his speech "Anything after but is bullshit. I got you, bae. When it's your turn, just be ready to show up." She pointed her index finger in his face, flaunting her freshly-manicured nails.

"My name wouldn't be Dooski if I didn't put on for my city," he boasted, then pressed his lips against hers.

"Show out right now." Myesha smiled mischievously, squeezing his dick. She leaned down, shoving her tongue down his throat. Moans and grunts filled the room as they swapped saliva.

BEEP! BEEP! BEEP!

Dooski jumped to his feet.

"Bae, that's yo' car?"

"Yeah, stay right there."

Myesha stiffened. Mentally she weighed her options. It didn't take long for her curiosity to get the best of her. She leaped off the bed and followed close behind.

Dooski opened the door and darted down the stairs. He could see a red Toyota Camry at a distance. He carefully examined his car. Nothing seemed out of the ordinary. Peering down at the gas tank, his brows crimped and his eyes tightened. There was definitely something up with his gas tank. He wiggled the side that was slightly raised and it effortlessly opened.

"Fuck!" he yelled, slamming his hand down on the trunk. Myesha appeared, dumbfounded. "This nigga done fucked my motor up!"

Myesha looked at him confusedly. "What nigga, Dooski?"

He stepped closer, invading her personal space. "I don't know. You tell me. You drive this bitch too. I know I'm not fucking around." He harshly jabbed his chest.

Appalled, Myesha's brow raised. "Really?" she questioned.

"Yeah, really!" he spat. The corner of his lip curled upward and he peered at her in disgust before walking away.

Ah'Million

CHAPTER 5
BOBBY

"Baby, what is this?" Bobby's grandmother held up the vegan burger closely examining it.

Bobby chuckled softly, amused at how she peered over the rim of her glasses. "Just try it, Granny, it's good."

She did so, taking a small bite. "Oh." She looked at it again as she chewed. "It is good," she added while taking another bite.

Bobby and his grandmother aimlessly conversed while enjoying their food. A little laughter here and there.

"Oooh, I'm full as a tick." She stood to her feet.

Bobby tossed a twenty dollar bill on the table and grabbed her by the hand. She waddled closely behind him. He made sure to walk slowly enough so that she could keep up. He waved to the waitress that had served him and eye fucked him the whole time before making his exit.

"Hold on," he said, then darted to the passenger side, opening her door for her. "Come on, Granny."

Ms. Taylor's sight was weakening by the day. It was strong enough to see things closely, yet it was the further things that ruffled her.

On their way back to his grandmother's, Bobby played a little Johnnie Taylor, known as JT. His grandmother only listened to two genres of music: blues and gospel. He chose blues most of the time. As a child, it vexed his spirit because it was the only selection of music his parents listened to.

"I want you to meet my dear friend Katherine down at the church."

"Okay. I'll go with you this weekend." Bobby's phone rang.

"Well, she's coming by today."

His phone rang. It was his alarm he set last night notifying him of Susie's shift ending. "I'm sorry, Grandma, I can't stay today. I have to go to work."

The glasses rested on the tip of her nose as she gazed in his direction. "Okay."

He led her inside and quickly helped her settle in.

"I love you, Granny. I'll see you later." He pecked her on the cheek, then headed for the door

"Bobby!" she called out from her sofa

"Ma'am?" He stopped, then turned around.

"Whatever is done in the dark comes to the light." She paused. "That's all I'm going to say."

Bobby stared at her, swallowing the lump in his throat, clinging on to every word. "Yes ma'am," Bobby responded before dragging to his car. He pushed his grandmother's words to the back of his mind and focused on the task at hand.

He rushed to Susie's jobsite, hoping she was still there. He arrived at the building ten minutes later. All Bobby knew was that she was a secretary at a law firm. He parked a few cars down from her Cadillac.

Luckily, she emerged shortly, appearing to be in a rush. Bobby watched her from a distance, shaking his head in contempt. *This nigga don't even have a type.*

Susie pulled off, and he wasn't too far behind her. Just like he hoped, she veered into the Exxon down the street.

Gotcha.

He pulled in shortly behind her. Susie was already darting inside of the store. Bobby parked and hopped out, not wanting to miss his opportunity. She was the third person in line from the register. He pretended to tie his shoe while discreetly stealing glances. Peeping her progress, he leaned up and headed inside, but not before colliding with Susie. His phone fell and hit the cement.

She gasped sharply. "I'm so sorry." She bent over and picked it up. She handed him his phone.

"Aww, man, look at my screen," Bobby voiced, pretending to be upset.

"Damn, that is the 13, huh?" Susie inquired.

"Sure is. Just copped it yesterday. You gon' have to get me another one of these," Bobby added.

"I don't ha-have that kind of money," she stumbled over her words. Fear was evident.

Bobby smiled. "Okay, I'll settle for your number than. That'll cover the expenses with your fine ass."

Susie turned red as a tomato, giggling like a young school girl. She brushed him off. "You're charming," she said, taking his phone out of his hand. She saved her number. "I'm Susie," she voiced walking away.

Bobby watched her with a smile plastered on his face until she was no longer in view.

Ah'Million

CHAPTER 6
KAD

"Pills on wheels!" one of the many men seated in the dayroom yelled.

You would've thought they said the first ten to the door would be released the way the men dashed towards the door. nearly stumbling over each other in the process.

Beep!

The nurse used the handheld device to scan the bands around their wrists to obtain they're medical information. Kad and Zip leaned against the wall, discussing a situation prior to today while keeping their eyes on everyone and everything in front of them.

"Man, Zip, pour a nigga up." Kad had been thinking about the potent drank ever since the day he took a sip. Zip wasn't lying. He'd managed to get pure codeine inside of the facility. Kad didn't give a damn how he got it or where he gotten it from. All he knew was that he wanted more. Since losing Danielle, Kad had taken a liking to the drink, which only he and Bobby knew about.

"Daniels!"

Zip and Kad looked in the direction of the nurse.

BOOM! BOOM! BOOM!

She beat on the glass, but the guy kept walking.

"Daniels! Let me see your mouth!"

He blatantly ignored her.

Daniels, who they referred to as Boy Boy, was known for selling his psych meds. Kad didn't understand what most guys got out of it, yet he knew they were getting something, since Boy Boy had commissary stacked to the ceiling. Hustling his pills was his only option if he wanted to eat since he had no money on his commissary account.

"Look." Zip pointed to the officers that were headed their way.

Kad bit down on his bottom lip as he eyed the beauty coming his way. The beat of his heart sped up the closer she got. He swallowed the lump in his throat as he watched her strut inside. Her name was Mayes - Lieutenant Mayes, to be exact. Her face held no emotion as she moved with purpose. Attractive when she wasn't even trying to be was what really turned him on. Everything about her was appealing, including the small shit, like whenever she would use her pinky nail to move her bangs away from her eye.

"Daniels!" She slid the door to his cell open.

Kad stared at her inviting back side.

"I see you looking at all that ass," Zip joked.

Kad grinned, lowering his head to hide his guilt. "Mmm, mmm, mmm" he murmured, shaking his head slowly. He rubbed his palms together. "She just don't know, man." Kad sighed deeply.

A few more COs rushed in to aid Ms. Mayes with her cell search.

"Mayes been a stuck-up bitch since I've known her." Zip sucked his teeth. "I knew the bitch when she was just a funky CO."

Kad nodded his head, but truthfully, he wasn't listening to shit Zip said. The only thing he wanted to hear was something flirty from the beauty before him.

"I'm writing you a contraband case and from now on, you're mandated to go to the infirmary to take your medication!"

"I don't give a fuck. Do what you got to do. I'm gon' still bond out and go home!" Daniels shot back.

"Nigga, please, you been here since Ice Cube was rapping. You haven't made bond yet. You're not going to make it." he tossed her hair over her shoulders and headed back out.

"How are you doing, Lieutenant Mayes?" Kad yelled over the chaos.

She stopped and whipped her head in his direction, locking eyes with Kad. The corner of her mouth curled upward instantly. Instead of speaking back, she simply nodded and proceeded to the door.

Kad smacked his lips. "She's still mad." He sighed deeply.

"For that shit you pulled when you first got here?" Zip asked.

"Hell yeah."

They both walked further into the dayroom and took a seat at one of the tables.

"Yeah, if you were cool, I would've laced you up about that one."

"It's cool, man, fuck all of that. Where the drank at?"

Zip flipped the toothpick upside down with his tongue and teeth while peering around from left to right. "On some real shit, I drank my last zone yesterday man."

"You drank a whole zone, nigga, and you didn't give me any?"

"I had been sipping for 'bout a week. That's what I gave you the other day"

Kad leaned in closer. "How can we get some more?"

Zip peered at him through slits. "You can't fuck this up, bruh."

Ah'Million

CHAPTER 7
JEWEL

Jewel's eyes felt like someone had placed quarters on her lids to prevent her from opening them. She blinked rapidly. The swelling had made them that way. After Bobby left the hospital last night, she wept until she fell asleep. Never in a hundred years would she guess she would experience such a catastrophe.

A single tear fell from the corner of her eye and into her ear as her present issues invaded her mental. The physical pain was mediocre compared to the mental and emotional anguish.

Whose baby is this? Should I tell Blotchy? It's a possibility the seed growing inside of me could be his. He deserves to know too.

Jewel was a hundred percent sure it was Bobby's though.

The screeching sound from the door grabbed her attention. Her heart stopped and her eyes widened in fear. She wasn't ready to face her fears. Not here; not now.

"Hey chick." Myesha grinned rounding the corner.

Jewel sighed, deeply relieved that it was just Myesha. However, as soon as the thrill died, envy ascended. Seeing Myesha's wide smile was uncomfortable as a size too small shoe. She had been faithful to Blotchy the little time they were together and was willing to show Bobby the same amount of respect, given the chance. *How is she so happy in her relationship when she doesn't even cherish it?* Myesha rushed towards Jewel and wrapped her arms around her neck. She buried her nose in her chest savoring the Versace perfume.

"You good?" She pulled back. Myesha was dressed in a cream-colored blouse, white high waist shorts, and a pair of gold Versace sandals adorned her feet. Her makeup was subtle, yet perfectly applied.

"Yeah, as good as it gets," Jewel replied with a half-smile.

Myesha ran her perfectly-manicured fingers through her long box braids. She winced in pain. "Oooh, these hoes tight. Them damn Africans don't be playing. You like them?" She turned in a complete circle. The platinum highlights enhanced her features.

Although Jewel wasn't too fond of her cousin's presence at the moment, she was relieved it was her rather Bobby or Blotchy. Seeing either of them would only terrify her even more.

Jewel stared at her cousin silently, then turned in the direction of the light seeping inside of the room. "Myesha, I'm pregnant."

"Bitch, what?" she shrieked. She rushed to Jewel's side and hugged her tightly. "I'm so happy for you!" Myesha jumped up and down. "Ooooh, bitch!" She bounced cheerfully. "I'm about to be a aunty and godmama! We got a lot to talk about. Let me go get some snacks." She turned to walk out, but ran into Bobby."

"Gushers please!" Jewel called out.

"Ooh, my bad. Hey Bobby," she greeted, almost colliding with him on her way out.

"How are you doing? You good?" he asked, seeming concerned, yet his eyes declared something else.

"Yeah. Before I forget, can I show you something real quick?" She held her hands up in surrender. I" know you're not here for that, but it's important."

"What's up?" His brows dipped in confusion.

Myesha whipped her iPhone out and within seconds, a hard beat blared through the speaker. The instrumental alone enthralled him and before long, he was bobbing his head to the tune. Bobby had no clue Myesha was indicating music, however, he was impressed and anxious to see what her lyrics were about. There wasn't a female signed under the label.

A male's voice erupted, killing his hopes, but not his interest. They had just dropped an artist. Picking up a new one was right up his alley. He lowered his head and listened carefully to the lyrics. His flow was not only unique, but profound He liked it – a lot.

Myesha paused the song. "You like it?" She grinned. She looked as eager as child on Christmas.

"Let me see that." He peered down at her phone. She handed it to him. "This all him right here?" he inquired, scrolling through the selection of music.

"Yep." She stood back, looking like a proud parent. She had swiped all of Dooski's music and saved it to her phone because she knew he had too much pride to approach him directly.

Bobby listened to another one, and then another one. "Who is this?" he inquired. There was no need to hear any more. Dude was hard.

"My boyfriend Dooski."

Bobby nodded his head slowly, remembering the night they first met. "I'm about to save my number. Tell him if he is trying to get to a real bag, hit me up ASAP." Bobby handed Myesha her phone back once she was done.

She covered her mouth in awe. She couldn't wait to share the good news with Dooski. "Jewel, look, I'm sorry, boo. I'll catch up with you later. I have to tell my man we are about to be famous!" she yelled, sashaying out of the door.

Jewel chuckled at Myesha's giddiness. Her smile faded abruptly once she locked eyes with an impassive Bobby.

He cleared his throat. "Jewel." He lowered his head. Shame filled him as if it was gas and he was the empty tank.

"Huh?" she responded, her voice a bit choppy.

He gritted his teeth, angry because his need to speak was dire. He was just unsure how to say what was on his heart, but he knew he had to say it because the pressure of withholding it was too strenuous, making it hard for him to breathe. "Aye." He looked at her, then up towards the ceiling.

She eased up in her bed, anticipating what was next to come.

He tucked his lips inside of his mouth as he thought of a way to begin. The only person he had expressed himself to was his grandmother. He couldn't fathom why he felt the way he felt. It was pestering him: the persistence, the constant tug at his heart strings. He turned to walk away, scratching his head. It didn't itch though. "Jewel, I, um…"

The door opened, diverting their attention. A nurse walked in. She wasn't the same nurse from last night. He was dying to see her again.

"How are you feeling?" she asked, peering from Jewel to Bobby.

Bobby's brow dipped in confusion. He'd seen her before. Maybe he was tripping. Perhaps he wasn't.

"I'm fine. Can I leave?" Jewel asked. Her head was throbbing and she was in dire need of a hot shower.

"Yes, everything is fine. Make sure you pick up your prescription. Good luck." She smiled before turning to walk away. "Are you the lucky father?" she asked, posted next to the door.

Bobby clenched his jaw. He may have been unsure at first, but he was definitely certain now. She was a friend of Kesha's - Kesha best friend, at that.

"That sounds a little personal to me, Miss…" He waited. His eyes narrowed into slits as he eyed her intently, waiting for her to confirm something he already knew.

Paranoia etched her face. She brushed her hair behind her ear. "I, I do apologize, that was very personal. I should get going." She lowered her head and made a swift exit.

"Let's go, Jewel."

CHAPTER 8
BLOTCHY

Blotchy pressed his foot on the gas as he accelerated through the light. He roughly tapped the screen on his phone, mumbling obscenities under his breath.

"You have reached the voice——" He flung his phone hard to the left, connecting with the window, cracking it instantly.

"Fuck!" He punched the steering wheel, gritting his teeth as he weaved in and out of traffic. He reached over and grabbed his phone.

"Hello?" Dooski answered in between laughter.

"Hey, where's Myesha?"

His urgency halted Dooski's laughter immediately. He cleared his throat. "She's right here. Hey, what's up?" Dooski questioned.

"Ask her if Jewel is still in the hospital."

"Oh nah, my baby said she left earlier."

Hearing him refer to Myesha as "baby" made Blotchy cringe.

"Bet." He hung up the phone before Dooski could respond. He figured since Dooski purposely left out her whereabouts, she wasn't with them. There was only one other place she could be.

Swiftly, he whipped his Charger around in the middle of the street. His heart rumbled in his chest while in pursuit to his destination. Drops of rain trickled down. Blotchy gripped the steering wheel tighter. The last time he followed Bobby home he was on pills, lean, and dro, but it didn't affect his memory. He was hoping he'd spot his car as he slowed and drove down through the residential area. However, instead of spotting Bobby's car, he spotted Jewel walking up the driveway and into the house. Blotchy hurriedly jumped the curb and parked in the middle of Bobby's yard.

"Are you fucking crazy?" Jewel shrieked, nearly dropping the food in her hand.

Blotchy walked up on her. His eyes locked on hers. She could feel his breath. "Yeah, crazy for you," he whispered.

She smacked her lips and looked away into the distance.

"Look, Jewel…" He reached out and grabbed both sides of her cheeks. "I want you back. I fucked up, alright? I know you and this nigga Bobby on some fuck shit, but I don't give a fuck." He spoke with so much aggression. His eyes searched hers as if he could find the answers in them. Blotchy gritted his teeth harshly. "Really, we can get out here and go for what we know. The last man standing wins it all." He spoke with determination.

Jewel lowered her head, unsure of how to respond. His words made her feel light, light enough to float. She didn't think he care, but he did. So she thought. "Um…" She moved her hair behind her ear. "There's no need to fight. Bobby is just a friend of my father's." She peered at the ground. "There is nothing going on between us" she continued to lie. She would lie a thousand times just to refrain from hurting him. Although he had hurt her plenty of times, she refused to return the gesture. She hated herself for lying.

"So what's up?" He threw his hands up. "Why he acting like that?" he pried, utterly confused.

"Why?" she mocked. Her brows dipped.

Blotchy's left brow raised He was curious to know.

"Him and my dad knows what the fuck you did to me." Her hand shook uncontrollably as she tried to regain her composure. She wasn't exactly sure if Bobby knew, but she did tell her father somewhat.

Blotchy lowered his head, pinching the bridge of his nose. "Jewel, I'm sorry" he voiced, lifting his head. He peered at Jewel unblinkingly, hoping she'd see his sincerity. "Now I'll never get a chance again with the label." He pinched both eyes. "Ross wanted to sign me, man. I had that shit right here!" He pointed to the palm of his hand.

Jewel's eyes widened in shock. "Ross?" she asked in disbelief.

He pulled out his phone and went directly to the messages where there was proof. She covered her mouth in awe.

"We were gon' be set, Jewel." Rejection laced his words.

"Well, what happened?"

"They found out about the accident we were in. He don't want no one in his label deeply involved in the streets."

"Damn."

"I'm gonna get going. I don't want to be disrespectful. Aye, label or no label, we gon' be straight." He leaned in and pressed his lips against hers. "I'll see you later," he said before turning and walking away.

Ah'Million

CHAPTER 9
BOBBY

Bobby parked his car in the driveway and hurried inside. He wasn't planning to be gone so long, but time flies when you're being slick. He and Susie had decided to meet up at Duck Creek Park in Mesquite. It was refreshing, minus the few minutes he spent convincing her to keep her clothes on. Kad may have been careless with his tool, but pussy was the last thing that moved him, especially from a bitch like Susie. She was the typical bunny that loved black pipe. Her lips were a lot looser than he thought. All Bobby needed was a night or two with her and she'd tell everything. In just forty-five minutes, he found out about her lousy marriage, big lawsuit, lame sex life, and rich husband on top of the different positions she found appealing.

"Jewel!"

"Yes?" she answered from the rear.

"Come here." He set the Chinese food down on the table and peeled off his Amiri jacket. His mouth watered as soon as he spotted her. Her thickness was completely exposed as she bopped toward him in the oversized T-shirt.

"Are you hungry?" he asked, pulling the chair out.

She nodded her head, grinning while clasping her hands in front of her. Although Jewel had just eaten, she'd eat ten more times if that meant receiving attention from Bobby.

"Hold on." He went to retrieve her a spoon from the kitchen. "What you want to drink?"

"You."

Bobby grinned boyishly. "Come on, for real, Jewel."

"I'll take water."

He poured her a glass of water. Opening the container, he placed the spoon inside and placed the napkins right beside it before sitting next to her. "Enjoy."

She dove in as he picked her left leg up and began massaging her feet. She couldn't believe he was showing so much affection.

"Come here," she called him with her finger. "Let me see if you got a fever."

He pulled away, bursting with laughter. He rotated feet while she ate and spoke in between bites.

"Bobby? Bobby," she repeated

"Huh? My bad, I was just thinking."

"Thinking about what?" She scowled.

"Nothing. I just zoned out." He placed her foot down softly. "Have you showered?"

"Yes, I did."

"Okay, cool, I'm about to hop in real quick." He stood and headed to his room.

Jewel stored her food in the refrigerator, humming songs along the way to her room to put on something sexy.

Bobby stood underneath the shower head, letting the steaming hot water pour down on him, removing the day's residue. He wished the hot water could remove a lot more than residue, like the mental anguish and emotional separation that he was enduring. He turned the water off and dried off, entering his room with just a towel wrapped around his waist.

He stopped mid-stride upon entering his room. Jewel lay bare on top of his sheets. The sight of her box alone made his man rock up, lifting the towel slightly. "Come on, Jewel, cover up. I know you not gon' just give me the pussy. Make me earn it. Have a little more class." He walked away and tossed his dirty clothes in the laundry. He returned and Jewel was underneath the sheets. He retrieved his clothes from his dresser and got dressed in front of her. His eyes trained on hers the entire time. Bobby wasted no time climbing into bed, gritting his teeth in the process. As he positioned the pillow Jewel wasted no time closing the distance.

"Bruh, come on." He scooted further away.

"Don't be like that, Bobby," she whined, wrapping her legs around his.

"Bruh, I'm serious!" He turned and faced her. "That's your side and this is mine! Stay on yours!"

Jewel rolled onto her back. Stiff as a board, she peered up at the ceiling, then slid soundlessly out of the bed. She picked her shirt from the floor and left the room, yet it didn't go unnoticed.

Bobby sighed deeply as soon as she left. He sat up, clasping his hands in his lap. His left leg shook uncontrollably.

"The fuck, man?" he whispered aggressively, slamming his fist against the sheet. He stood to his feet, clenching his fist. "It's not even worth it."

He wanted to walk into her room, apologize, and love on her, but his mind, body, and soul were on two separate accords.

"Come on, Bobby," he murmured. Pain shot through his jaw from the amount of pressure he applied gritting his teeth. "Loyalty is rare. Don't put yourself out there to get hurt."

Harshly raking his hands through his hair, he pinched the bridge of his nose. "Nah. Nah, man," he whispered, marching towards the door. Finally, he had gotten his feet to move. He reached for the knob.

Once you get involved that's it. Once you find out she's still fucking around, you're going to be ready to kill or be killed. If something happens to you, what will happen to Granny?

Liquid burned the back of his eyes, yet it wasn't nearly close enough to fill them. He aborted the mission and returned to bed. During his prison stint years ago, he lost his father. A love greater than life itself, his father was his hero since he was old enough to know what a hero was. Every day he lay awake on his bunk, regretting the decision to go with Kad that night, because he wasn't even able to honorably lay his old man to rest. His pops never missed a PTA meeting, a game, or any sort of function involving Bobby, but Bobby missed the day that held the same significance as the day he was born. He wasn't even able to console and comfort his mother. He was released only to lose her too. The guilt enveloped him like a gush of water and he vowed to never commit or conform to anything that would take his independence. Some nights were more pestering than others. He thought he would completely lose the sanity he had left. Then there was his grandmother, the only piece of family he had left, his only peace, trust, and comfort. He owed her everything.

Bobby climbed under the sheets and closed his eyes, but sleep never came. He tossed and turned until he simply couldn't lay there any longer. He sat up and peered at the clock on his nightstand

4:55 a.m.

Bobby retrieved his laptop out of his dresser and located his playlist. The Gospel blurred through the speakers.

"I'm praying God comes and turns this thing around. God turn it around, God turn it around, God turn it around

I'm calling on the name that changes everything. God turn it around, God turn it around, God turn it around.

'Cause all of my hope is in the name,

The name of Jesus.

A breakthrough will come, come in the name.

The name of Jesus..."

Bobby bobbed his head to the lyrics, humming along to the song as he got dressed. He needed to speak with the man upstairs, but he wasn't responding, so that left one other person.

* * *

"Hey G'ma." Bobby walked inside, closing the door behind him.

"Hey baby." She grinned, exposing her gummy smile. "You're here early."

"Yeah, I know. I brought you a donut, latte, and some fresh fruit." Bobby knew his grandma's daily routine like the back of his hand. He knew she'd be awake. She was a woman of God and never missed a morning of prayer and bible reading with the man upstairs.

She picked up her dentures and put them in, then leaned all the way back in her chair. Her arms folded across her chest and her glasses rested on her nose.

Bobby picked at the pig in the blanket. It smelled amazing and looked even better, but with the shit that weighed heavy on his heart, it restrained him from doing the simplest things, like eating. Oblivious to the lingering stare, Bobby finally peered up, hearing his grandmother clear her throat.

He swallowed the piece of food in his mouth. "Ma'am?" He looked at her through eyes of discontentment.

"Boy, what's wrong with you?" Her eyes narrowed into slits.

He shook his head. "Nothing, Ma."

"Who are you fooling, Bobby? I'm not crazy. You hardly ever come over this early. Look at you. You can't even eat. Give me that."

Bobby chuckled, handing his grandmother the barely touched pig in the blanket.

"I don't know how to love. I won't allow anyone close to my heart, afraid that my loyalty could possibly keep me from you."

Slowly, she stood and wobbled to the sofa and flopped down next to him. "Let me tell you something." Her plump hand covered his. "Once you've asked God for forgiveness, it is tossed into the sea of forgiveness and forgotten. God, forgave you, boy, now forgive yourself. Don't harbor that blame and guilt. Your mother and father wouldn't want that for you. They'd want to see you living your life to the fullest potential. Love and be loved. Be fruitful and multiply." A single tear glided down her cheek as she gave Bobby her famous smile that he cherished so much.

"Yes ma'am." He cracked a smile.

Bobby enjoyed the company of his grandmother a little while longer, giving visitation at the Dallas County Jail enough time to begin. Around eight, he left and headed out to see Kad. Taking his grandmother's advice, he tapped the Door Dash app and sent Jewel breakfast, hoping she'd accept it with an open and forgiving mind. He sat in the parking lot until it arrived and sent her a text.

Bobby: My apologies for last night, love. I hope you enjoy the breakfast.

He sent the text and strolled inside. There was plenty he needed to catch Kad up on. On his way up the flight of stairs, he took the money out of his pockets and stuffed it in his sneakers.

He bypassed the COs while heading to the desk. Confusion etched his face along with anger that surged through him. Both he and Blotchy locked eyes until the lady at the desk snatched Bobby's attention.

The fuck he doing here?

Bobby gritted his teeth as the thought of Blotchy visiting his homie came to mind. Kad never was the sucka type and he hoped he wasn't becoming one. His leg shook uncontrollably as he waited for Kad to emerge. Shortly, he did. Kad couldn't even pull out his chair good before Bobby went in. Squinting, he licked his lips before speaking

"Aye bruh, Blotchy up here to see you?"

Kad returned the same scowl. You would've thought he swallowed a ball of salt with the expression he wore. "Hell nah. I don't fuck with that dude. Why you think I told you to cut his bitch ass off?"

Bobby sighed deeply, relieved to hear the opposite of what he assumed.

"Why, what's up? Is that what he told you?" Kad asked, ready to pop off.

"Nah, we just bypassed each other on my way up. If it wasn't you, it was somebody." Bobby eventually dropped the topic regarding Blotchy and continued telling Kad about his interest in Dooski, progress with Susie, and everything else other than his relationship with Jewel.

CHAPTER 10
BEY

Stuffing the chocolate bar inside of Dooski's gas tank wasn't enough, so she plotted more trouble.

"Why haven't you been answering my calls?" Bey questioned Brandi as soon as she entered the small apartment she and her sister once shared with their mother.

Brandi strutted casually towards her mother. She dropped her Versace bag on the sofa and flopped down onto the worn cushion.

"You hear me?" Bey continued.

Brandi rolled her eyes, then slung her long bundles over her shoulder. "Bey, I got this. Different shit been coming up and it's prolonging things."

Bey glared at her daughter intently. *I could just strangle her ass.* "Oh so you think you're hot shit?"

"Nah, you think I'm hot shit," Brandi shot back.

Bey sat up in her seat, pointing her finger in Brandi's direction. "You not gon' keep disrespecting me in my shit."

"Your shit! Exactly! Look at this place. You called me over here." Brandi clapped in between words. "I got my own shit. I stopped depending on you a long time ago. You're disrespecting yourself! Look at you! This nigga got you looking like a heroin addict!" She paused, inching closer. "You're not dope sick. You love sick!"

"You can leave now," Bey spoke through clenched teeth. If there was a slight chance that she would possibly get away with killing Brandi, she would have definitely taken it.

"You don't gotta tell me twice! You're not going to ever change. Steady allowing these men to abuse and misuse your own." Brandi turned around and snatched her bag up. "You are lucky the pay good. No telling what you did to get that."

Bey leaped up out of the raggedy loveseat. "Get the fuck out and call me once the job is done!" Bey yelled.

Brandi scowled in disgust. "You think I'm scared of you?" she asked, tossing her bag onto the sofa.

KNOCK! KNOCK! KNOCK!

Both of their heads whipped in the direction of the door. Bey went to open it, lightly brushing Brandi in the process. Brandi bit her lip while nodding her head slowly.

"What are you doing here?" Bey asked, staring into the eyes of her oldest daughter.

Bianca brushed past her and into the apartment. "Mother and daughter date?" Bianca asked Brandi.

Brandi sensed the sarcasm instantly. "Nothin' like that. I'm just trying to get a bag."

"For real!" Bianca whipped her head in her mother's direction. "Bruh, I told you to dead that shit!" She walked up on her mother. "That's your seed, Ma!" She looked at her through eyes of distaste. "You're losing your fucking mind, dawg!" She turned around. "And you…" She pointed her finger in Brandi's face. "That's our little sister! That's a baby, B!" she voiced aggressively. Her eyes bucked like she had just snorted an ounce of dope.

Brandi smacked her lips and waved her sister off.

Bianca mushed Brandi hard in the face, causing her to lose her balance and land on her ass.

"Bitch!" Brandi scurried to her feet.

Bianca whipped her .45 out of her bag and held it by her side.

Brandi slowed down, peering up at her sister in disbelief.

"Yeah, stud up if you want to." She cocked her burner, then inched closer. "On God, I'm going to burn ya ass if you harm my li'l sister," she continued, then tapped her against the forehead with the barrel of the gun before walking away

"Really, Bianca? We ran away together, fought, stole, starved, and ate together. You don't even fuck with her like that," Brandi reasoned.

Bianca stopped, then turned to face Brandi. "Didn't I protect you, bruh?" She peered through narrow slits. "Huh?" Brandi nodded her head. "I got fucked in every single hole, every fucking night, just so you'd get by with just sucking dick instead of taking it. I even tried to stop that from happening," she voiced breathlessly. "We all share the same thing," she continued, then paused. "And that's blood." Tears brimmed in Bianca's eyes. She swiped them away before turning and walking away, leaving the door to the apartment open.

Bey sighed deeply, then dragged to her seat. She watched Brandi wipe her face while gathering her things.

"Look, I understand if you want to end the mission." She sighed deeply. "Maybe I need to go make amends with your sister and ask her for forgiveness."

Brandi sniffled, then turned and faced her mother. "Fuck Bianca and her threats. I'm all about a bag. You gon' either get rich or die trying, and we going to go someday." She dropped the invisible mic and walked out the door. She gripped the knob, then turned to face her mother. "I'll text you when it's done. Just Cash App me the rest of my money."

Bey nodded in response and once she was sure Brandi was gone, she smiled mischievously, then reclined in her chair.

Ah'Million

CHAPTER 11
JEWEL

Jewel listened to Myesha praise and brag on Dooski through the Airpods while getting ready for night school. She had only one more class until graduation, and she was eager about it.

A text came through her phone grabbing her attention.

Blotchy: Can I take you to school?

Her heart raced in desire. All she longed for was a little love and affection, and at the present moment, she felt deprived. Bobby was the guy her soul yearned for. However, he made her feel terrible for feeling that way because all he managed to do was make her feel unwanted. Questioning who she was as a woman had become part of her daily routine.

"Jewel!" Myesha yelled repeatedly into the phone.

"Huh? My bad, girl."

"What are you over there doing?"

"Look, I need a favor." She sighed deeply.

"What's up ?"

"If Bobby calls you and ask you anything, tell him I'm with you."

"I can do that, but where are you going to be?"

"Well, I'll be at school, but Blotchy wants to take me out so I'm going to let him pick me up too."

"Oh, okay, bet, yeah, I got you. Let me call you back. My sister on the other line."

Jewel ended the call with Myesha and before she could set the phone down, another call came in. She grinned and picked up the call.

"You have a collect call——" She quickly accepted the call.

"Hey Dad."

"Hey baby girl, what you doing?"

"I'm on my way to night school."

"Oh, that should be almost over, right?"

"Yep, two more to go and I'm done."

"Okay, that's good news. Look, I need you to do something for me."

Jewel carefully listened to her father's instructions. It was different than most tasks, but she'd go to the moon and back just to show her father that she was no longer that little girl.

She finished her hair and got dressed. She didn't want to apply too much makeup and cause Bobby to question her intentions, so she settled for something a bit subtle. She dabbed on a coat of gold eye shadow - a bronze gold, nothing too bright or shimmery - then her mink lashes. She dabbed a little concealer under her eyes, then a coat of lip gloss.

Her screen lit up. Blotchy was right on time. She quickly gathered her things and headed outside. Bobby would kill her if he pulled up now.

"I got you something," Blotchy said as soon as Jewel slammed the door shut. He handed her the Panda Express bag.

She grinned with excitement. He knew how much she loved Chinese food. "I'm about to tear this up right now," she said, opening the container. "You have a plastic fork?"

"Yeah, it's one in the glove compartment."

Jewel opened it and spotted the fork with a small box on top of it. She peered at Blotchy, dumbfounded.

"Oh yeah, that's yours too." He smirked.

She opened the box. Jewel covered her mouth in awe. The tennis bracelet glistened immaculately inside the palm of her hand. She had never seen so many diamonds at once, and the gold trimming only made it more intriguing. She reached over and wrapped both arms around his neck, burying her head in the crease. The Versace cologne assaulted her nostrils, sending some sort of electrical wave to her pussy. Her box throbbed like a mean migraine. She pressed her plush lips into his.

Immediately, he opened his mouth and invited her into his. He slid his tongue inside of her mouth and danced with hers. Their tongues slowly danced, breaking every so often to exchange deep pecks and a bit of lip slurping, Jewel slowly pulled away, remembering where she was, but not wanting to reveal her level of fear if caught.

They both enjoyed the positive vibe the entire ride to the school. Jewel managed to eat nearly all of her food while laughing and conversing along the way.

"You going to pick me up?" she asked Blotchy before closing the door to his car.

"Hell yeah, whatever you want me to do."

"Boy, you be gassin'," she joked, closing the door.

"I'll show you better than I can tell you." He winked, then pulled off.

Jewel spotted Kesha as soon as she entered the classroom. She wasn't sure if word had spread, but all eyes were on her. She gave them all a "what" expression, making them turn their heads.

"Five minutes until class, ladies," the teacher announced.

Kesha' eyes stayed trained on her. It was as if the announcement was on cue. She stood and made her way towards Jewel. Jewel sighed deeply.

"Hey Jewel. Jewel, is it?" she asked, portraying to be dumbfounded.

Jewel put on her fakest grin ever. "Yes, it's Jewel."

"Bobby told me all about you," she lied. "I'm so glad you pulled through. He loves you more than anything."

Jewel peered at her strangely. *This bitch is weird.* "He said that to you?" she asked.

"Yes. He told me that he and your dad have been cool for years and although he don't have kids, he loves you like his own." The statement dripped with sarcasm.

"Yeah, yeah th-that's right." Jewel lowered her head and rushed to her seat. Her heart raced with trepidation. She wanted to buck and handle the situation like she would any situation where she felt offended, but she didn't know Kesha, and the last thing she wanted was for Bobby to be in a cell next to her father facing sex charges.

She must think I'm a fool.

Jewel tried her damndest to focus on her teacher and the scribble behind her on the dry erase board, yet it was difficult. Her mother's words rang loudly in her head.

"Honey, whatever you do in the dark comes to light."

As a child, she didn't understand the idiom. However, approaching adulthood, she understood there was no way she was going to be able to live two different lives. Things were bound to surface.

The vibration from her phone interrupted her thoughts.

Blotchy: Time moving slow asf, but it's cool, I'll be able to see your sexy ass in 20 minutes.

Jewel blushed as she envisioned him saying such silly things. She texted him back and put her phone back in her bra. Unintentionally, her eyes met Kesha's. She seemed to be glaring at her. However, Jewel had other things to worry about. She whipped out her phone and quickly texted Bobby.

Jewel: Myesha is picking me up.

"Five minute break, ladies," she announced.

Kesha flew past her and down the hall.

Bobby: Bet.

Jewel sat the last few minutes in class, admiring her new bracelet until the bell rang.

"Good night, ladies. I'll see you all Thursday for the final class before graduation."

Jewel quickly gathered her things. She couldn't wait to thank Blotchy all over again. She tossed her bag over her shoulder and held her folder in her hand as she moved swiftly down the hall.

Her smile faded as she neared the glass door that stood in between her and the wintry night. It was Bobby. *The fuck is he doing here?* Jewel instantly began to panic, backing away from the door.

"Hey, that's your uncle. Do you need a ride, or you got your own?" Kesha smiled.

Immediately, Jewel sensed the bitterness that laced her words. "I'm good. I'm waiting on my ride."

"Cool." Kesha turned around and opened the door to leave, but peered back at Jewel before leaving completely out. "You sure? You don't need to be waiting up here like this."

"I'm sure."

Honk! Honk! Bobby rolled his window down. "Kesha, come on, I don't got all day!" he screamed.

Blotchy veered into the lot shortly after. Jewel gave Bobby time to pull off, then exited the building and climbed inside the car. She silently prayed Bobby didn't notice Blotchy's ride. He leaned over and met her with a kiss as soon as the door closed. Moans filled his Audi coupe.

"Jewel, where's one place, at this present moment, you wish you could be."

Jewel 's smile faded before she lowered her head. "Umm…" She sighed deeply. She knew her desire was unrealistic, but she voiced it anyways "I wish I could be with my mother."

Blotchy looked away, instantly remembering her difficult casualty. Like a light bulb, the idea surfaced instantly. "We can do that. Where's the gravesite?"

* * *

Blotchy pulled into the lot near the gravesite. He removed his seatbelt and opened his car door. He placed one foot on the gravel, but then stopped, noticing her lack of movement out the corner of his eye.

"What's wrong?" Jewel appeared to be in deep reverie. "Jewel?"

"Yeah, yeah, I'm cool," she said, opening the door.

"You've been here before, right?"

"Yeah, it's just that this time it's a little different. I've never gone with anyone other than my dad."

"Come on." Blotchy met her on her side, grabbing her by the hand. She gripped it tightly as the burst of cold wind slapped her in the face. "Hold on." Blotchy scurried back to his trunk and pulled out a thick and colorful quilt and stuffed it in his backpack before tossing it over his shoulder.

Jewel's brows dipped in confusion.

"This is what I use whenever I get stuck at the O." He locked hands with hers and dragged her forward. He spotted the chains from a distance. "What kind of shoes do you got on?" he asked with her in tow. He veered around to the side. He tossed the backpack over first. "Go first."

The fence appeared to be anywhere between ten and twelve feet tall. Jewel grabbed the fence and wasted no time working her way up and over.

"Ugh!" she yelled, landing on her feet.

Blotchy laced up his shoes, then pulled up his jeans. He stuck the burner deeper into his briefs before gripping the cold metal. He hopped the fence with expertise.

"I'm scared, Blotchy," Jewel whispered, taking ahold of his hand. She clung closer. She had never visited the gravesite at night, in fear of the gruesome things she had heard and seen on TV.

Blotchy removed his burner, clutching the steel with his left hand, then wrapped his arm around Jewel with his right. It sounded like they were fiddling with a potato chip bag as they moved slowly through the cemetery, crushing the leaves beneath their feet. The lack of wind eased the discomfort from the low temp. It was more of a stale cold than anything.

"It's the big one right there." Jewel pointed.

"Come on," Blotchy whispered, placing his hand on the center of her back, slowly urging her forward.

"Hold on." He slung the backpack off his back and unfolded the quilt. He sat against her mother's tombstone, comfortably propping himself against it.

Jewel peered around into the dark, caressing her forearm for a brief release from the cool air.

"Come on, bae."

Blotchy's legs were spread wide enough for Jewel to sit in between them, and she did. She scooted backwards, pressing her back against his chest. He lifted the quilt and draped it over the both of them.

"You good?" he asked, tucking the quilt underneath his legs. "I got something else for you, big head."

Jewel chuckled softly. "Hmm, and what is that?"

He unzipped the backpack and removed a box of Gushers.

Jewel grinned, exposing all of her whites. "I love these!" She immediately opened the box.

"I have two more in here for you too."

The small gesture made Jewel's heart smile.

The flickering sound caught her by surprise. Blotchy set the lit candle on the side of the tombstone. The sweet aroma brushed her nostrils instantly. The fragrance was familiar. "Ocean," she whispered low enough so that Blotchy couldn't hear. It was her father's favorite.

Blotchy leaned back, wrapping his arms tightly underneath her breasts. He sighed deeply. "Hey Mama. I'm Blotchy." He sighed again. "I just want to thank you for this beautiful woman. I promise to love and protect her as long as I have breath in my body and even when I die when I'm merely a spirit." He paused, then cleared his throat. "I'll keep her safe, and alert her whenever danger is ahead." Blotchy brushed her stomach with his fingertips.

Jewel held her breath, hoping it'd slow her racing hear, afraid to expose her true feelings. *Why is he doing this all of a sudden?* Caught up in her own thoughts, Jewel had forgotten the task at hand.

"It's your turn, Jewel."

Oh Lord, she pondered aimlessly, unsure of exactly what to say. Jewel was a ball of emotions as she gritted her teeth to refrain from teary eyes, yet they still fell. Her chest rose and fell as her lip began to tremble. She missed her mother; she missed her father. She finally felt love from someone other than her parents, yet she carried another man's seed. Along with the bundle of emotions, she felt unsure of where, who, and how they stemmed.

"Shh, shh." He grabbed her by the face, slightly turning it, then pressed his lips against hers. His breath was a mixture of sugar and spice. He sucked and slurped, roughly then changed the pace, planting pecks and lightly brushing his lips against hers. "Calm down," he whispered into her mouth

"I can't. I'm sorry," she sobbed.

Blotchy eased the already-rolled blunt out of his pocket and put fire to it. He hit the weed and passed it to Jewel. Within minutes, she was laughing and speaking freely.

She was on the second box of Gushers when she asked Blotchy, "If you don't mind me asking, how did your younger brother pass?"

Blotchy sighed deeply. Jewel grabbed his arms, wrapping them tighter around her.

"Well..." He cleared his throat. "When I was thirteen, my mom kicked me out of the house because I got at her dude. But I only did that because he treated her so badly." He gritted his teeth. "He, um... He had no job, no hustle, no nothing. All he would do was lay around while my mother provided everything. Well, once I got kicked out, I would hang out in different places around the neighborhood, and once it got dark, like a little bit before midnight, I'd go home and my little brother would let me in through the window. I would change clothes, take bird baths, and then do it all over again. In the midst of it all, I was stealing from people and stores just to survive.

"This particular night when I went home, I kept looking back 'cause I had this eerie feeling, but I didn't see shit so I paid it no mind. Well, I got to the crib and went through the window, and Anthony went to close the window down." He paused, wiping the tears from his face. "Next thing I know, BOOM! BOOM! Two shots hit him hard. The first one in his chest and the next one in his throat. Killed him before he fell."

Jewel gasped sharply before swiftly turning around and wrapping her arms around his neck. "Oh my God, Blotchy!" she sobbed.

He cried silently. He lowered his head. "It was all my fault. I must've burned the wrong nigga. To this day, I still don't know who smoked my little brother." He appeared to be in a trance.

"Shh, don't do that." She squeezed him tighter.

He sobbed into her chest until there were no tears left.

CHAPTER 12
MYESHA

"This is cute, huh?" Myesha asked Dooski as they lay in bed gazing at the screen.

"Bae, you don't even know what she's having."

She turned to face him. "I know, but I really like it. I'm going to buy it just in case." Since finding out about Jewel's pregnancy, Myesha had gone nuts buying all sorts of things. The Dior bibs had caught her eyes. They were beyond irresistible, and she refused to pass them up.

RING! RING! RING!

"Hello?" she answered, never taking her eyes off the screen.

"Bitch, what's up, what you doing?" It was Brandi.

"Cuddling with my nigga. You okay?"

"Yeah, I'm good! Bitch! I got this lick. All I——"

Myesha interjected. "You didn't know?" Myesha scowled.

"Know what?"

"My nigga just signed with New Money Ent!"

"That's what's up!"

"Nigga, we made it!" Myesha blurted before erupting with laughter.

"Damn, so what? You acting funny now 'cause yo' nigga up?"

The phone went silent as Myesha thought of a comeback.

"You can't count anybody's money but yours, honey. The second you become dependent on a nigga is the second you're gon' have to buy you a shovel to dig yourself up out of that hole."

Discreetly, Myesha cut her eyes at Dooski. *She's right.*

"I know your sucka ass is over there thinking that Dooski isn't like the rest and he'll never do you like that, but bitch, you can sleep when you dead. You better stay woke on these niggas."

"Okay, okay, sis, quit crying," Myesha voiced, pretending to soothe the person on the other end of her phone. She hated to admit it, but Brandi was right. "I'm getting dressed right now. Myesha sounded hysterical, in an attempt to convince Dooski. She hurriedly ended the call and jumped to her feet.

"Bae, what's going on?" Dooski asked, jolting forward. He did exactly what she wanted him to do.

"Brandi's dude just ran up in the house and started swinging on her!" she lied.

Dooski's brows dipped in confusion. "The fuck wrong with him?"

Myesha shrugged. "That's what I'm ready to figure out." She laced up her Jordans and dove across the bed. She planted kisses all over Dooski's face.

"Bae, we gon' go grab a bite to eat while I let her get everything off her chest."

"Bet. Bring me something back," he said.

He wrapped his big arms around Myesha and squeezed her tightly, and at that moment, she wished she could remain right there in his arms forever. Even though Brandi had a valid point, her faith in Dooski effortlessly outweighed her doubt. He was genuine, and she didn't base it off shit he told her, but signs he showed her. However, fear would make someone doubt their own capabilities.

* * *

Brandi had been trying to convince Myesha for the last thirty minutes. Myesha didn't mind the dancing gig, but she wasn't up for anything outside of that. Today she was in no mood for any other man but her own. Stripping and fucking were two different things. Her pussy was sacred.

"You acting funny," Brandi sneered.

"No I'm not, I'm just not feeling all of that!" Myesha wanted to take back what she said, but it was too late. She had already snapped.

"Cool. Fuck you. I'll go by myself. We not on the same type of time, so I'll just take you back," Brandi shot back, slamming her foot against the pedal. She weaved around the other cars carelessly.

"Brandi!" she whined.

But Brandi continued to drive like she was on *Fast and the Furious*.

"Brandi!" Myesha repeated twice more.

The flashing of the lights bounced off the side mirror. Before they could react, the opps was behind them, announcing his presence.

WOOP! WOOP!

"Fuck!"

Brandi didn't know if she should slow down or speed up. She had an ounce of soft in her glove compartment.

"What the fuck are you doing? Stop!" Myesha peered at Brandi in bewilderment. *This bitch is crazy.*

"Look, sis, I'll stop, but you gotta take that for me," she pleaded with her eyes trained on the road, swiftly peering in Myesha directions after every word.

"Take what?" Myesha asked. Her heart fell to the pit of her stomach. She was afraid of what Brandi would say next. "W-what?" she stammered. Brandi didn't answer. Myesha palmed the dash. "Answer me, goddammit!" she yelled. Her eyes widened as her veins protruded from her neck"

"Chill! You won't even spend a night!" Brandi protested. "Look, I got a little dope in my glove compartment."

"Hell nah!" Myesha interjected before Brandi could finish.

"Come on, sis, I got two dope charges already." Tears filled her eyes and fear dwelled in the pit of her stomach as Brandi's left leg shook uncontrollably. Her head swiveled swiftly from left to right.

"Fuck! I knew I shouldn't have come with you, bruh! Why would you even have that shit in the car and you knew you were coming to pick me up?" Myesha pointed at her chest. Her eyes were bloodshot red as she swelled with pain and frustration.

"Put your hands where I can see them!" the officers yelled, rushing to the car.

Myesha gritted her teeth as the tears fell two at a time. Flashlights and guns drawn, they forced both of them out of the car.

"Get out of the car now!"

Seated on the curb, Myesha cursed herself as she thought about how upset Dooski was going to be once he found out.

"Please, sis," Brandi begged in a low tone.

The glare Myesha shot her way was given to someone you despise. Myesha's heart raced while the policeman searched the vehicle. She held her breath, hoping he wouldn't find anything, but so much for wishful thinking.

"Now I'm going to give you an opportunity to tell me whose this is, or both of you are getting charged." He held up the Ziploc bag full of white powder.

"It's——" Myesha started mentally preparing for what was next to come.

"It's hers!" Brandi screamed, predominating Myesha's soft voice.

Myesha glared at her, appalled. You would've thought Brandi had two heads.

"Is this yours?" The officer inched closer without taking his eyes off Myesha.

She responded, "Yes sir, it's mine."

CHAPTER 13
BRANDI

BOOM! BOOM! BOOM!

Brandi backed up away from the door after hysterically beating on it. Dooski opened the door. It was evident he had been asleep.

"Why you beating on the door like that? Why y'all just…wait," he continued, rubbing the sleep from his eyes.

"She's not with me," Brandi spoke up. Her confidence dwindled by the second.

"Where the fuck she at?" It was like Dooski had been on drugs mere seconds ago and on the drop of a dime, he had sobered up. His beady eyes were as wide as golf balls while he stood there panting like some sort of animal.

"Ugghhh!" Brandi wailed in frustration. She buried her face into the palm of her hands and bulldozed her way past Dooski and inside of the house "We were eating when she saw this dude she used to know." She flopped down on the couch. "They left me at the table while they left to talk. Well, when she returned…" Brandi paused, retrieving a piece of tissue from her bra, and dabbed at the corner of her eyes. "She told me she was leaving with him."

"Who the fuck is him?" Dooski asked, enraged. His bottom lip trembled as if he was shirtless and standing outside in forty-degree weather.

"I don't know, I've never seen him before."

"Bruh, quit lying to me!" He stood just inches away from her face. His eyes had turned bloodshot red, and the veins in his neck and forehead protruding, causing the pace of Brandi's heart to speed up.

Damn, this nigga tripping.

"Fuck this. I'm about to get my bitch." The corner of his lip curled upward as he sized her up before walking away. He removed his T-shirt and headed to his bedroom.

Water filled Brandi's mouth as she ogled the muscles in his back. Brandi bit down on her bottom lip. *Think, bitch, think.*

She ran after Dooski and into his bedroom. You might want to reconsider," Brandi suggested watching him rummage through his closet.

Dooski ignored her and continued with what he was doing. He found what was looking for and stood to his feet. She eyed him unblinkingly as he walked out of the closet shirtless.

He a little chubby, but I don't give a fuck.

"They found dope in the car, Dooski. It was a lot. I could tell by the way the officer held the bag." She paused, flopping down on the bed. "She took the charge, Dooski, and they knew she was lying. They knew she was covering for someone. If you put your name on her bond, I wouldn't be surprised if they question you."

Dooski's brows dipped. The shit he was hearing was beyond bizarre. The last thing he wanted was a dope charge. "Really? This bitch took a dope charge?" He brought his hand down over his face. The frustration was evident. He slung the clothes across the room and flopped down on the bed. "Fuck that bitch. She dead wrong," he voiced, punching the air.

Gotcha. Brandi smirked, then altered her expression before turning to face him. "I mean, if you want, I'll do it. We can go half on her bond," she suggested, pretending to express sincerity.

"Bruh, you go get her out. Tell that nigga she left with to give you half of the money."

"Come on, Dooski, don't be like that." She inched closer.

"I'm dead ass."

She took the already-rolled blunt from her bra and put fire to it. One of her tricks had given her the ounce of gas. "Here." She extended her arm, placing the perfectly-rolled blunt in plain sight.

He was angry beyond measure, but he knew good weed when he smelled it, and there was no way he was going to pass it up.

"Fiya, huh?" Brandi grinned, watching Dooski as he inhaled the potent drug.

Dooski didn't even respond. He just passed it back. Joy in any form would be the last emotion expressed after finding out the disturbing news.

"Why you didn't stop her from going with that nigga?" he asked through squinted eyes.

She hit the weed, buying time to respond correctly instead of irrationally. "I can't tell nobody grown what to do, Dooski," she voiced in between tokes.

"You right. I'm gon' dead that shit." He stood to his feet.

Brandi handed him the blunt and he walked out of his room. Seconds later, the sounds of pots clanging and cabinets slamming could be heard throughout the house. She peered around dumbfounded, then left to peep the scene.

Dooski had meat, seasonings and other condiments on the counter.

Brandi chuckled "What are you making?"

"Shit, I'm hungry. I'm about to make some tacos."

"Boy, you don't know how to burn."

"Watch."

She flashed him her freshly-manicured nails. "I'm cool," she said.

Dooski shrugged. He hit the weed twice more and tossed it into the garbage disposal. "You got some more?" He turned to look Brandi in her eyes, which was the first he had done so since answering the door. He was no longer tense and belligerent. His eyes were glazed and lax, and the only thing he desired at the moment was more of the euphoric feeling that he got from the potent weed.

"Yeah," Brandi answered, raising her brows.

"Roll another one."

She leaned a tad bit over the counter with her hands clasped under her breasts, exposing her cleavage.

"Only if you let me stay for tacos."

Dooski's eyes fell on her breasts, then back up to her eyes. He shrugged, then turned back around.

Brandi smiled mischievously, then went to retrieve her purse. She would've gotten on all fours if he would've asked her. *Myesha don't know what to do with a nigga like this.*

Brandi removed her jacket and kicked off her gold heels. She took it upon herself to put on some music as she rolled the blunt.

"Drugs got me sweatin' but the room getting colder
Looking at the devil and the angel on my shoulder
Will I die tonight? I don't know. Is it over? Looking for my next
high. I'm looking for closure.
Lean with me, pop with me, get high with me if you rock with
me.
Smoke with me, drank with me
Fucked up liver with some bad kidneys..."

Brandi bopped to the music as she went inside the kitchen to pass Dooski the rolled blunt. He seemed to be enjoying the music as well, waving his arms over the stove like he was at a concert.

"Eyes red, no Visine
Crash the Mustang, no saline
Yeah, I love P's, yeah, I love lean.
I laugh when they ask is my piss clean.
Smoke with me, pop with me,
Gucci store, come and shop with me.
If I overdose, bae, are you gon' drop with me?
I'on even want to think about that right now.
Let's get too high, reach a new high."

He sang the lyrics loudly as he jigged to the beat. There was no doubt that he was using the music to express what he was truly feeling. The song came to an end and so did the vibe, Brandi decided to give him a helping hand, but not before handing him the bottle of Jose Cuervo

"Here, go chill, I'll finish that," Brandi suggested.

They locked eyes for a moment longer than intended. His honey-colored eyes were as contagious as COVID, and definitely dangerous too. There was no way she could have his heart when it belonged to someone else. All the caution signs were boldly exposed, yet Brandi had no fucks.

She brushed past him, slightly grazing his dick along the way. He peered back at her, but Brandi kept stirring the ground meat, ignoring his presence. She decided to make a little rice on the side. She opened the counter and grabbed the brown rice. She nearly jumped out of her skin when she met Dooski's face after closing the cabinet.

"Oooh, you scared me," she whispered, placing her hand over her heart.

He roughly pressed his lips against hers, cupping her juicy ass cheeks and lifting her on top of the counter.

An abundance of things went crashing against the tile. Moans and grunts filled the kitchen. Swiftly, they struggled to free each other's hidden jewels. Brandi helped Dooski. She tossed her shirt to the other side of the room and dove back in. Their lips never parted. They were locked as if they held some sort of magnetic force while still trying to remove the piece of clothing they had left. Dooski's pole was as stiff as cement and he was ready to poke something.

Brandi lifted her ass cheeks off the counter to help Dooski remove her leggings. He didn't even bother trying to remove her thong. He simply ripped it apart. As he tossed the underwear behind him, a foul odor brushed his nostrils, yet it didn't slow or stop his stride. The sight of her plump cookie made his penis throb. He yanked his gym shorts down in one swift motion. His pole leaped up like it had springs in it, and the sight alone gave Brandi anxiety that Xanax couldn't lighten. Dooski pulled back, using the back of his hand to rid the saliva around his lips.

"Give me some top." He backed away, slowly stroking his tool. Perspiration covered his forehead.

She couldn't wait for it to drip onto her skin once he long stroked her kitty. Brandi jumped off the counter and dropped to her knees. She grabbed his pole with two hands and went to work. Wrapping her heart-shaped lips around his tool, she sucked and slurped while using her hand to choke his dick. Veins protruded from Dooski's neck as he gritted his teeth to refrain from grunting. He reached out and held onto the counter, feeling his legs buckle.

"Shit" he whispered, panting for air. He placed both hands on each side of her face and roughly pumped his pole down her throat.

Brandi's sinister laugh vibrated the tip of his pole, making him shudder a bit. He kept thrusting, and she enjoyed every second of it. Tears leaked out the corner of both her eyes, but it was all tears of joy.

"Mmmmm!" he sounded. His dick was so far down her throat that her nose was pressed against his pubic hairs.

After emptying every drop down her throat, he finally loosened the grip he had on her head. He tapped his pole against her forehead, ridding whatever was left. Brandi grinned, then turned around and grabbed her ankles. He backed up just a little bit, lifted his foot, and kicked her square in the ass.

Brandi fell so hard onto the floor that the tile seized a thin layer of skin from her knee. Appalled, she scurried to her feet. "What's up with you?" she asked from the opposite side of the room. Her face distorted with confusion as her chest heaved rapidly.

"Don't act dumb. Get your shit and get out." Dooski pulled up his briefs and shorts and started picking up the things off the kitchen floor.

"So that's it?" she voiced through slits.

"You not my bitch. Don't question me, dawg."

"Fuck your fat ass then!" she yelled, putting her clothes back on

"Before you try to fuck something, get your pussy in check!"

"My shit stay in check," she shot back, offended by his statement .

He threw the ripped panties, hitting her directly in the face. "Yo' shit smell like dog breath. Get the fuck on."

Brandi had never met a nigga that denied her, and although she was hurt, she didn't show it. Fully dressed, she grabbed her purse and left, slamming the door in the process.

"Don't slam my shit. You know I wasn't gon' fuck you, bruh! Right idea; wrong dude!"

Hot tears covered her face before she even climbed inside of her car. She felt humiliated and exposed like a cheap prostitute who had just got fucked in every hole and kicked out of the low budget suite.

It wasn't even about the dick. He had verbally degraded her like no other.

Angrily, she whipped out her phone and shot her mother a text.

Brandi: It's done. Send me my money.

Ah'Million

CHAPTER 14
KAD

"Good visit?" Zip asked as soon as Kad sat across the table from him in the dayroom. He didn't want to appear anxious, but he was curious to find out who Blotchy came to visit.

"Fa sho', everything is everything. What about you?" Kad wanted to know if Zip had a visit, searching his eyes for any leery movements. but from the looks of his creased scrubs. there was a strong possibility, indicating a sure sign he had been to a visit.

Zip sighed deeply with a boyish grin on his face. "It was good, it was good. That was my li'l shawty. She twenty years younger than me, but we are more compatible than any woman I've dated my age."

Kad cracked a smile as his eyes shifted swiftly in every direction. He wondered who Blotchy could've been visiting. Zip could have been telling the truth.

"You good, youngsta?" Zip inquired, peering him.

Hesitant, Kad carefully considered his response, afraid to expose too much. Zip was cool, but trust was something that had to be earned. However, something about these circumstances surpassed his ego and instead of sticking to the script, he changed it a tad bit. He pushed his beliefs to the side and granted his innocence until he could prove Zip was guilty.

"I'm straight. I just don't trust mu'fuckas so I'm on edge, but it's cool."

Zip appeared offended. "Me?"

Kad cleared his throat.

Zip leaned in closer. "Look, I wouldn't put you in any situation that I wouldn't put myself in." Zip's gaze was firm and potentially intimidating.

Yet Kad was far from average. His eyes matched his level of intensity, displaying his stiffness without verbally expressing it.

"You already in some deep shit. We here, bruh," Zip continued. He stretched his arm above his head, exalting his level of loyalty.

That's my baby girl.

His mind drifted to their conversation prior to the one today. He felt a hint of every emotion you could possibly feel once she was done talking. He was irate, but his circumstances hindered him from acting like a petulant child. There were things he had to definitely see about, but unfortunately, it would have to wait.

"Check this." Zip leaned in. "In the morning, they're going to call you to medical. Be ready."

Kad smiled and gritted his teeth, rubbing his hands together. "Alright, bet."

"Y'all look like y'all up to no good," Lieutenant Mayes commented, hovering over the table in which they sat. She and Kad locked eyes. Hers weren't flirty, but soft. A half-smile etched his face. He found pleasures in the gesture since she always looked past him instead of at him. However, the glare she shot Zip would've put him out of his misery if it had been a gun. Zip's mug wasn't friendly either, making it a bit awkward.

The fuck?

Later that night, Kad and Zip sat amongst a group of others watching the game between the Celtics and the Heat. Kad hoped the Celtics would win. He felt they'd be more competition for the Golden State Warriors. A commercial emerged and chatter erupted.

"Zip, you never told me how your visit went," Loc voiced.

Kad was zoned out, thinking about the play tomorrow. Zip cut his eyes at Kad, then Loc. His eerie silence grabbed Kad's attention. He eyed Zip out the corner of his eyes, then back to the screen, yet the shit on the TV was his least concern.

"Rack it up!"

Kad and the rest of the men didn't budge, a look of perplexion on their faces.

"I said rack it up!" CO Johnson repeated.

The group of men blurted a barrage of obscenities.

"Shut up, fuck boy," Zip uttered.

"Pussy ass," Loc commented

"Gay ass."

Loc finished his canned drink. Kad emptied the rest of the chips in his mouth. Both of them tossed the trash on the steel table.

"Take your trash with you!"

"Fuck you!" Loc shouted.

"That's yo' job!" Kad shot back.

Zip chuckled, in pursuit to his cell.

"Y'all youngstas wild!"

Kad nodded, yet he was mentally devising a plan to catch Loc and ask him about Zip's visit.

Ah'Million

CHAPTER 15
KESHA

It was a few days before Kesha's graduation ceremony and she hadn't heard a peep from Bobby. Her once-flat abdomen had begun to protrude and she was regretting the decision of keeping Bobby's seed. After finding out she had lied about her car the night she asked him for a ride, he cursed her out and then remained silent - the usual. She knew it was all because she had made his precious Jewel feel some sort of way. Since that night, she had tried a hundred different ways to miscarry the seed growing inside of her, but nothing seemed to work. Not yet.

Ring! Ring! Ring!

Monica arrived with a grin that would lighten the worst mood, yet it only darkened Kesha's. She looked around in horror at Kesha's place. The smell that assaulted her nostrils was worse than a prison segregation cell.

"Why is it so dark up in here?" she asked, high-stepping over shit on the ground. The light hurt Kesha's eyes, but the sight of her friend hurt Monica even more. Tears filled her eyes and she felt great sympathy for her friend. Kesha lowered her head, afraid to look into Monica's Eyes.

"How did you get here, Monica?" She peered up at her through moistened eyes. Her lips trembled as she rocked back and forth, waiting for a response that she knew Monica surely didn't have an answer to.

Monica rushed over to Kesha. She wailed like a wounded dog. Monica pulled away, gripping Kesha's shoulder. "No, no, no. No! If I got to be that baby's father, you're having that baby!" she spoke through clenched teeth. "Do you hear me?" She shook her.

Kesha's eyes were full of agony and exhaustion, but with the acceptance and security spewing from her good friend, she had no choice but to be strong. Kesha nodded her head in agreement.

"I want to hear you say it, Kesha." Monica leaned in closer, her lips almost touching hers.

Tears fell, continuing to stain her cheeks. "I am going to have this baby."

"Louder, dammit!"

"I'm having this baby!"

Both of the ladies erupted with laughter, embracing each other tightly.

"Come on, girl." Monica stood with her hand out, helping Kesha off of the floor. "You sure have gained weight," she said, breathing heavily. "How many months are you?"

"A little over seventeen weeks."

"Damn, where does all the time go?"

"Look, go make us a drink while I clean this place up." Kesha slid right past her. "Aye, and make sure your shit is virgin."

She smirked at Monica.

They joked and talked aimlessly while cleaning and enjoying each other's company.

"Girl, I haven't had this much fun in a minute. I got to start getting out." She flopped down on the sofa.

"I'm not done." Monica rolled her neck. "Throw some clothes on. We gots to get you ready for this graduation."

"I don't graduate until next week," Kesha attempted to protest.

"It's cool. If you need a touch-up before then, we'll do that."

CHAPTER 16
JEWEL

"Hello?"

"Hey, I'm a friend of Myesha and she asked me to call you so that you can set your phone up."

Jewel jolted forward. "Set my phone up?"

"Yeah, she's in Dallas County"

"Okay, tell her I'm doing it now!" She hung up the phone and called Dooski. It went straight to voicemail. She tried calling again, and this time he forwarded her call

Motherfucker!

She ran out of her bedroom, frantically searching for Bobby, but he was gone. Remembering the instructions, she immediately started the phone process. She searched the web to find out Myesha's bond.

Ooooh shit!

"One hundred and fifty thousand," she mouthed in awe. Her heart raced as thoughts of Myesha being locked up surfaced. She hadn't heard from Myesha in nearly a week, but that pattern had become normal since getting with Dooski and hanging out with her sister. The last place she would've looked was the county.

RING! RING! RING!

The 1-800 number flashed across the screen and she quickly answered.

"You have a collect call from——"

Before she said her name, Jewel accepted the call. "Hello?"

"Aaagghh!" Myesha screamed in joy. "Oh my God! I've been trying to call you for a week!"

"Bitch, tell me everything! Don't leave out nothing."

Myesha went on to tell Jewel everything that had happened leading up to the moment she got arrested.

"Girl, I can't believe Brandi's bitch ass! I'm going to call her as soon as this phone hangs up!"

"Nah, let her be. I'm done with that bitch. I don't want any further dealings with her."

"How are we going to get you out? Your bond is high as hell and Dooski isn't answering."

"It's a bail bond down the street that'll take seven percent, which is eleven to twelve thousand to get me out."

Tears filled Jewel's eyes. She didn't have that type of money. "I don't have it like that since my dad got locked up. I can try and see what I can come up with," she said, feeling inadequate.

"You have one minute left," the operator cut in.

"Try for me, please. Ask Bobby, if need be, and Dooski will pay him back. I don't know where the fuck he's at. Please don't leave me here. Get in touch with my baby and let him know I'm here."

"Okay"

"Goodbye," the operator announced.

Tears fell down Jewel's cheek as she pitied Myesha's circumstances and possible future. Her cousin was like her best friend. She couldn't lose both her and her father to the system.

She called Dooski twice more, but got the same results. She called Brandi just to find out she had changed her numbers.

Her phone vibrated. It was a text form Blotchy.

Blotchy: I need to see your beautiful face. I'm on my way.

That's exactly what she needed: a distraction. She dried her eyes and got dressed to see her man. Although they were not official, neither of them were concerned with a label. They simply enjoyed the time spent and looked forward to spending more time together. She and Bobby had been spending more and more time away from each other, which made Jewel's life a little less difficult. Bobby even seemed nicer than usual whenever he was around. Jewel figured that it was because she was giving him space rather than suffocating him. Although every day Blotchy was stealing small fragments of her heart, storing it in his pocket, her love for Bobby was still solid as a rock. However, she was done with trying to convince him.

The loud music snapped her out of the trance. She made sure everything was in place then grabbed her purse and ran outside.

She climbed inside his car. His smile was so warm and inviting.

"Hey baby." He grinned, flashing his pearly whites.

"Hey." Jewel was elated.

He slowed then stopped at the stop sign and their lips merged instantly. Jewel didn't want to disrespect Bobby by any means, so she made Blotchy comply with a few rules. Pulling away for air, she shot Bobby a quick text.

Jewel: I'm with Myesha. Be back in a few.

Right then and there, it dawned on her. If she asked Bobby for the money and he found out she was in jail, how would she be able to get away with Blotchy?

I can't ask Bobby, but I can't leave my girl hanging either.

Blotchy stopped and grabbed a few boxes of pizza, soda, and two boxes of breadsticks from Papa John's. Today they would keep it simple and Netflix and chill.

"Bae, what's wrong? Why you so quiet?" Blotchy asked as he parked outside of his apartment.

"I'm just thinking about something." She flashed him a tight-lipped smile before lowering her head.

Blotchy grabbed her by the chin, lifting it into his direction. "Can we talk about it?" She sighed deeply and nodded. "Come on," he urged, gathering everything out of the car.

Jewel removed her shoes and got comfortable on the sofa. She wanted to remove her hoodie, but was afraid Blotchy would see her bump that looked more like a curb with each passing day. He snuggled up next to her, passing her the pizza just how she liked it.

"Here you go."

Jewel eased the pizza from his grasp. It was a slice of cheese and pineapple pizza with two cinnamon rolls stacked on top, just the way she liked it

"You have a memory like an elephant." She grinned.

"So tell me what's going on," Blotchy suggested in between bites.

Drinking the orange Fanta to wash down her food, she sucked her fingers then sighed deeply. "Myesha locked up."

Blotchy's brows dipped in confusion. "How long has she been in there?"

"About a week or so."

He scowled, wondering why Dooski hadn't told him. Jewel promised that she'd stay away from Blotchy and never speak to him again as long as her father promised not to do anything that'd jeopardize his freedom. Kad didn't agree to not jeopardize anyone else.

"How much is her bond?"

"One hundred and fifty thousand.

"Damn! What she—— It don't matter. See, bae, if you could convince your pops to go ahead and sign me."

"I can't do that, Blotchy," Jewel intervened.

"Come on, bae. Do it for us. They gon' give me a sign-on bonus and I'm going to chunk you whatever you need for your girl."

"Okay, I'll talk to him ASAP."

He hugged her tightly and Jewel flashed a tight-lipped smile. She knew the outcome, but it was still worth a try.

CHAPTER 17
MYESHA

BEEP!

"Not yet," the commissary lady announced after scanning the band on Myesha's wrist.

She smacked her lips, picked her nearly-empty bag from the ground, and dragged back inside of her cell. She had been so worried about bonding out she had forgotten to ask Jewel to put money on her books. Today was the day of Jewel's graduation and she didn't want to bother her knowing that she was somewhere prepping.

She returned back to the dayroom and flopped on top of the stool. Today made it two weeks, and she was already exhausted with the routine.

A chick that was booked in yesterday walked by, her bag loaded with goodies to the top. A bag of chips fell and Myesha picked them up and placed them on top of the chick's bag. Myesha watched her walk away, wishing that it was her. She had heard of jail and even knew a few people inside, but one thing she definitely witnessed for certain was the harshness of doing time with no support.

It's cool, I know Jewel gon' put some money on my books.

Betrayed was an understatement since she still hadn't heard a peep from Brandi's lying lips.

These bitches on here so ratchet.

"Aye." It was the girl that had dropped her chips. A hint of her makeup was still applied. Her lashes and brows were on fleek. The long and expensive lace front made her look exotic and her baby hair fell perfectly around her edges.

Damn, she's pretty.

"What's up?" Myesha responded, swallowing the lump in her throat.

She took a seat. "I'm Asia." She paused. "I don't mean to be nosy, but I heard you on the phone yesterday"

"Yeah, what's up, what about it?" Myesha's brows dipped in confusion.

She leaned up in her seat. "Yesterday I heard you mention Brandi, and I know a Brandi. Now that I'm looking at you, I do see the resemblance. Do you know Bianca?"

"Yeah, Brandi and Bianca are my sisters, but that hoe Brandi is dead to me."

"I'm just curious, 'cause I see that you didn't make store. See, me and Bianca like this." She held up her hand, her index and middle finger entwined. "She can't possibly know you in here because that bitch got that trash bag money."

Myesha grinned as the chick praised her sister. "Well, we are not as close as we used to be." Myesha's smile faded, then she lowered her head.

"I didn't ask that. That bitch show more love than TRAPBOY Freddy does on holidays, so I'm sure she doesn't know you in here going without."

"You right, I don't think she knows."

She stood to her feet. "I'll be back."

Myesha watched Asia use the phone from a distance and after a few minutes, she returned.

"She told me to tell you she's on her way."

"Okay." Myesha nodded, but she didn't believe it. She would have to see it to believe.

Her biggest disappointment was Dooski. She was sure that he knew by now. He was the last person she expected to switch up. Even if he didn't know before, Jewel definitely told him by now, yet he was still missing in action. If the shoe had been on the other foot, she would've scammed, sold mouth, pussy, and ass to get him out. But everybody ain't a real one.

Asia left and returned shortly with arms full of snacks. "Here, snack on this until they call you to pack up. My bond is being posted too, so if I leave before you, you can have that, then disperse all of that other shit."

"Thank you," Myesha said, grabbing the cakes and chips. She ate until she fell asleep.

Someone nudged her awake. Myesha stirred from her deep slumber. It was Asia.

"Huh?"

"They are calling you. Pack up!"

She wasn't bullshitting.

Myesha leaped up off her bunk and held Asia tightly. "Thank you so much. I thought I'd never get out."

Asia grinned. "You good. Tell your sister I'll see her in a few, and you stay your ass out of trouble. Cute bitches don't go to prison."

Myesha chuckled, then said, "I got you."

The release process took almost an hour, but it was all forgotten once Myesha opened the doors to freedom. The fresh air was better than a piece of pussy to a nigga on lock.

Honk! Honk!

She spotted the white Hellcat Charger and jogged to it.

"Thank you so much, sis," Myesha said, climbing inside. Bianca appeared a little irritated, so Myesha kept it short.

"You welcome. I wish I would've known sooner. We gon' stop and eat so you can tell me what happened."

Ah'Million

CHAPTER 18
DOOSKI

"Big Sam told me when they painted you a picture
  "Don't let 'em paint you another (Why?)
  Sayin' I switched sides, but you fuck with who tried to get me hit
  Fake friends smiling in my face, wanna send it at my top..."

Kevin Gates's "Broken Love" lyrics blared through Dooski's speakers. Although Myesha had played him close, he missed her dearly. There were days he'd be home alone and smell her scent or hear her laugh. He missed all the good and bad.

The ringing of his phone interrupted his thoughts.

"What up, Looney?"

"Aye, bruh, Blotchy ain't picking up. I'm over here at Rochester Park and ole boy bragging 'bout that shit he pulled at the red light."

"Oh yeah?" Dooski gritted his teeth.

"Yeah, and he talking about sliding again. Me and my guy going to follow him once he leaves the park. Make 'em eat all that hot shit he popping.

"Say less."

In less than ten minutes, he pulled up to the smoke shop. Blotchy's car was parked in the usual parking spot.

"Aye, Looney say ole boy bragging 'bout getting at you. Over there in the south pooping big shit."

Blotchy walked from around the counter. "Looney shouldn't have even been able to tell you that." He paused. "He should be busy silencing the nigga."

Dooski tucked his lips inside of his mouth in frustration. "Bruh," Dooski started.

"When did you become so concerned?" Blotchy peered at him through narrow slits.

Dooski scowled, looking him up and down, baffled. "What do you mean?"

"I saw ya car at Bobby's house. What's that about?" He crossed his arms

"He signed me."

Blotchy were prepared to hear anything but that, and his expression revealed it. "You?" he shot back in an attempt to humiliate Dooski.

"Yeah, me."

Blotchy erupted with laughter. However, inwardly he was filled with rage. "Oh, so you're my replacement? You just gon' step on my toes?" he continued. He knew his shot was good as dead now that he had been replaced.

"Bruh, cut it. You told me yourself you found something better."

"But you s'posed to be my dawg. Where is the loyalty?" He threw his hands up in the air.

"Loyalty? Bruh, you supposed to be my dawg and I couldn't even get a feature. I begged you to put me down." He jabbed his finger in his direction. "You selfish! You don't want anyone to outshine you!" Dooski continued screaming like a madman.

"That's bullshit. I eat, you eat."

"Yeah, as long as you are the one bringing the food to the table." Dooski's chest heaved like he had been running a race.

"It's always been fifty/fifty with us. I don't owe you or no other nigga a motherfuckin thang." Blotchy turned and walked away.

"Whatever, nigga! The money changed you, B!"

Blotchy stopped and turned around to face him. "Just know I don't fuck with friends of my enemies."

CHAPTER 19
BOBBY

Bobby had been ripping and running for the past few hours to make sure everything was perfect for Jewel's graduation. Indeed, he had been slacking intimately, but he vowed today to make a change. His mission with Susie had been completed, so now he didn't have to commit so much time and effort into the project. After a few strokes and cheap gifts, she was ready to marry a nigga.

The few weeks he had spent recording with Dooski, he realized that he was a bit more talented than Blotchy. He was very open-minded and versatile. He accepted criticism like a bad bitch would compliments, and most of all, he wasn't with all of the street beef shit.

"Jewel!" he called out from his room. He sprayed his Versace cologne on different areas of his body and picked one of Jewel's presents. "Jewel——" Her beauty ceased his speech as she emerged from her room. He boldly eyed her up and down, swallowing the lump in his throat. "You, um…" He paused, scratching his head. He licked his thick lips. "You look beautiful."

Jewel tried her damndest to control her breathing, but it was difficult. Her cream-colored dress fell a few inches above her knees. Her swollen breasts looked perfect sitting over the brim of the V-cut neckline. Although her baby bump was on full display, she looked fucking amazing. Bobby wasn't a big fan of makeup, but she rocked that shit.

"I, um, I got something for you before we head out."

"Okay." She smiled.

Damn, she sexy!

Bobby reached into his pocket and pulled a box out of each one.

"Open this one first," he said, handing her the shorter bow. For the first time he noticed the nice piece of jewelry around her wrist, and off instinct, he grabbed her wrist. "What's this?" His anger elevated.

Jewel eyed him foolishly. His death grip baffled and scared her all at once. "My dad bought me this," she lied, yanking her arm back. It was a lie, but then again it wasn't because Kad did buy her one - just not that one.

Bobby calmed instantly, softening his honey-colored irises. "I'm sorry. Well look, this one will go on your other wrist." He smiled as he placed it on her wrist.

"Wow," she whispered in awe. It sparkled like a chandelier. "This thing looked like it cost a fortune," she blurted.

"Nah, maybe a mortgage, but not a fortune." He chuckled. "Turn around." He inched closer, closing in the little space left between them. His semi-erect dick now pressed against her backside. He reached around her and secured the necklace around her neck.

She gently picked up the pendant. Jewel's mouth fell open in awe, then immediately, tears brimmed in her eyes. Bobby cleared his throat.

"It's just sixteen carats. I know the number sixteen is significant for you. Danielle was sixteen when she had you and you were sixteen when you lost her to the disease."

It was a breast cancer symbol formed into a platinum pendant, embellished with pink diamonds.

Swiftly, Jewel turned around, grabbing both sides of Bobby's face. Simultaneously, they leaned in. Their mouths merged roughly, yet it was the sweetest thing either of them tasted. It was impulsive and passionate. Their tongues emerged. Moans and grunts filled the room. Bobby leaned in further, forcing Jewel to take steps back. The wall ceased her movement as she balanced herself against it, embracing Bobby's pleasurable attack. He picked her up effortlessly by her waist and carried her to the nearest bedroom. Neither of them had yet to come up for air. With their lips still locked, Bobby managed to hike up Jewel's dress and remove her underwear. With just one hand, he eased his jeans down, releasing himself. His dick was stiff as a pole as he inched closer and tapped against Jewel's opening. Jewel lay on her back spread eagle, her perfectly-shaved the box on full display. She eased her freshly-manicured nails down to her kitty, instantly locating her love button. She eased down further into her tunnel, coating her index finger before slowly massaging her button. Biting down on those heart-shaped lips, she moaned softly.

"Give me that dick, zaddy."

Bobby climbed on top, then worked his way in and moved from side to side while making his way completely inside of her warmth, instantly regretting all the days he let pass without getting his fix. Jewel dug her nails into his back, her chest heaving underneath him as her screams filled the room. Pulling out and turning her over, Bobby wasted no time diving back into her warm, wet, and tight center. Spreading her ass cheeks, he dug deeper and deeper.

"Ooohhh, Bobby!" she cried, her head buried into the sheets muffling her cries.

Bobby slowed his pace, feeling a current building from his toes. He entwined his hands with Jewel's while stroking her slow and deep from behind.

"This my pussy, Jewel," he whispered into her ear, causing Jewel to shudder from the neck. He sped up. He knew he was on the verge of a buss, nothing less than euphoric.

"AAAAHHHH!" he sounded. Everything went limp.

Faintly, Jewel lay underneath him in complete bliss. She simply wished she could kiss him and start their sex session all over again. Unfortunately, she had a graduation ceremony to tend to.

"Bobby?"

"Hmmm?"

"Bae, we have to get to the graduation."

"Shit! You right." He spoke urgently, yet he moved slower than a turtle.

It took about twenty minutes for them to put on the same clothes he had tossed to the side. Finally, they were on their way.

Jewel's eyeliner had smeared a bit. Using the mirror on her phone, she fixed it effortlessly.

"I'm going to be late, Bobby, and it's all your fault" she joked, applying more lipstick.

He grinned. "No you not. According to the GPS, we should be there in seven minutes. It's ten minutes until four."

Ah'Million

CHAPTER 20
MYESHA

"Hey, let me call you back," Bianca spoke into the receiver as soon as she accepted the call.

Myesha could tell that it wasn't a usual brunch date as she watched her older sister move with a purpose. Everything about Bianca screamed boss. She smelled like one, looked like one, even displayed it in her strut and speech. Myesha peered at her through eyes of admiration.

"Table for two," she requested, her head swiveling swiftly around the restaurant.

Myesha would've preferred seafood, but Mexican food was cool too. On The Border was actually one of her favorites since she was younger. Bianca tapped her foot impatiently while waiting to be seated.

The fuck is going on?

Myesha couldn't understand why her sister was so antsy.

"Follow me." The lady led them to a table merely a few feet away beside a window.

Myesha took a seat, then glanced around at the semi-packed restaurant. It was the emptiest she had ever seen it. Bianca tapped her screen quickly.

"What would you like to drink?"

"I'm fine." Her response was quick and harsh.

Myesha gave the young and pretty waitress a tight-lipped smile, discreetly apologizing for Bianca's rudeness.

"Um, you can give me a pink lemonade."

"Okay. I'll be back to take your order."

The waitress disappeared. Bianca and Myesha locked eyes for the first time since picking her up from the jail. Myesha found it quite absurd that things had become so awkward between the two of them. She silently dwelled on the days when they were extremely close, before she and Brandi moved out.

"Okay, here you go." She placed the tall, thick glass of lemonade on the table. "Are you ready to order?" She looked at Bianca, then Myesha.

Timidly, Myesha peered at Bianca, hoping she'd contain her rudeness.

"Do ya thang, sis," she voiced, peering at Myesha. "I'm having whatever she's having." Bianca turned her attention to the waitress before diverting her attention back to her phone.

Myesha placed the order, sending the waitress on her way. "I think I'd make a good waitress," Myesha voiced as she watched her walk away, smiling at the idea. She had sold her body, drugs, dreams, and anything else she could make a dollar out of. She was ready to finally be legit.

"Now that she's gone, let's hear it." Bianca dropped the phone on the table so carelessly it made a loud, thud sound.

"Hmm… Where do I begin?" she asked no one in particular. "Um…" Myesha began to tell the story from the moment Brandi called her.

"Did you just say Brandi?" Bianca scowled. Disgust etched her face. Bianca wasn't as pretty as Brandi, but her confidence topped the baddest bitch.

"Yes, our sister Brandi," Myesha confirmed.

The moment the name rolled off of Myesha's lips, Bianca simply couldn't believe her audacity, after she warned Brandi. Refusing to jump to conclusions, she comfortably leaned back, clasping her hands on top of her lap, ready to hear the rest of the story.

"Okay, finish."

Myesha was finished telling her story. The food still hadn't arrived.

Bianca slammed her palm against the table, causing Myesha to nearly jump out of her skin.

"I told that bitch!" She jumped to her feet and grabbed her purse. "Come on." She turned around, nearly colliding with the waitress. "We gon' have that to go," Bianca demanded, pointing towards the front. She stormed through the restaurant, tossing her purse over her shoulder in the process.

She pissed, Myesha thought, seeing Bianca's clenched fist.

Bianca turned around abruptly, then pulled a wad of money out of her bra. "Here, go pay for the food. If they ain't ready in five minutes, leave it and we'll go someplace else." Bianca darted for the door.

Stunned, Myesha watched her sister walk away. Luckily, the waitress was on point. She arrived shortly with the food in the to-go plates. Afraid to irritate her sister even more, she handed her the fifty   dollar   bill.   "Keep   the   change."

"Oooh, thank you!" the waitress called out.

Myesha was already at the door.

"I'm glad you out, bitch. I need you to call Brandi's phone. She not answering for me," Bianca voiced, weaving in and out of traffic.

That must be Asia.

Myesha didn't even bother to ask where they were headed. The sun was beginning to set and Bianca had turned off the chilly AC and let the windows down. She wished the strong winds would blow her burden away and on top of all the drama, she missed Dooski.

You never know someone's value until they're just a memory.

A nudge in her side brought her back to planet Earth.

"Huh?" She slightly jumped.

"Girl, you didn't hear me calling you?"

Myesha lowered her head. "My bad. I, I was——"

"Look, it doesn't even matter. Where ya clothes at?"

Confused, Myesha said, "At the apartment I share w——"

"Fuck that nigga. He couldn't even post your bond. That's alright." Bianca swerved left, making a U-turn at the intersection.

Myesha wanted to protest. Bianca didn't know Dooski like she did. *Maybe I don't know him either.*

She remained quiet. She could talk until her face turned purple in an attempt to sway her sister about how good her guy was, yet actions spoke louder than words.

They pulled into the driveway of a two-story house. *Damn, this how sis doing it?*

The area was nice and quiet and her lawn was perfectly trimmed. She was impressed. She followed Bianca up the walkway and into the house. The inside was immaculate. The living room resembled a bar straight out of the seventies, sort of mimicking a vintage theme. Red carpet, lounge chairs, and multiple Black Heritage pieces hung sporadically. The seventy-inch plasma really set it off. Myesha was so busy admiring the place that she hadn't realized Bianca's disappearance until she appeared from the rear, tossing clothes in her direction.

"See if you can fit that."

Myesha held up the minidress, clearly dumbfounded. "What? Where we going?"

"I'm about to go whoop this bitch, but you can't slide with me looking just any kind of way."

CHAPTER 21
KAD

"McVale, you got a visit!"

He peered down at his watch, baffled. For one, it was late, and for two, he had spoken to Jewel and Bobby earlier that day. Today was her graduation. She wouldn't have had time to set up a visit.

He slid on his crocs and bounced. Kad had gone from a nobody to a someone in a matter of days. Indeed, respect was given due to the way he carried himself, but suddenly everyone wanted to be in his mix.

Kad sat with his legs wide open on the stool, fidgeting with the hairs on his chin. He focused on the door, waiting to see who would come through it.

It's probably Bey's ass, asking for more money. He didn't have the time nor money to contribute to her madness.

Suddenly, Sierra appeared. He could see her face though the small window attached to the door. He gritted his teeth as she appeared through the door, then stood off to the side. Kad remained seated.

Her smile faded. "You're not going to stand up and give me a hug?" she asked, stunned by his rejection.

"Bruh, sit down." Kad turned to face her, leaning onto the table.

"What is your problem?" she asked, clearly offended. "Is this how you treat someone that's down for you?" Devastation laced her words.

"See, I was going to give you the opportunity to tell me the truth." He paused, standing to his feet. "But you bop your ass up in here lying." He turned to walk away. "If you don't know, you'll find out soon."

"Nigga, I don't got to lie to you. That grown-ass man that's fucking your daughter is the one lying to you."

Kad stopped dead in his tracks. He swallowed the lump in his throat. Heat rose from his toes and stopped in the center of his chest, instantly ceasing his breathing. Jewel had told him about her unwavering attraction to the man he considered a brother, but she failed to mention that. Surely, she should've mentioned that.

He quickly gathered his composure before turning to face her. The last thing he wanted was for her to see him bothered. Honestly, Sierra didn't know if Bobby and Jewel were fucking or not. She figured if she was in Jewel's position, she'd be fucking Bobby, or desperately trying to. However, after making the threat to Bobby and him leaving her in peace, she figured there must have been some truth to it.

"Anything dealing with mines, I know what's going on, just like I know your slick ass is after my paper." He inched closer, invading her personal space. "But bitch, you gon' have to put me in the dirt before you get my shit." He walked away.

"I got you, nigga!" she blurted.

"Don't go back to my office!" he yelled.

"Fuck you, you ole weak-ass nigga!" Sierra screamed. She fussed and yelled obscenities until the officer escorted her out and down the hallway.

***

"You good, boy?" Zip appeared in Kad's doorway.

He lay on his back with his arms beneath his head, pondering over the bickering between him and Sierra. The thought of a grown man fucking his daughter tore a hole through his soul that not even a miracle from God could fill.

"I'm good," he responded dryly. He quickly rolled over on his side. "Aye, let me ask you something, Zip."

Zip leaned comfortably against the door frame. "What's up?"

"You got a little girl?"

"I got one."

"How old was she before you let her start dating?"

Zip lowered his head and chuckled. "I mean, she grown now, but, um, I didn't."

"Damn, Zip, so how did that work out? Do she have kids? Or is she a nun?"

"Well, actually, that unrealistic expectation cost me." He paused. His eyes fell to the ground. He raised his head, then cleared his throat. Kad thought he spotted a glimpse of gloss in his eyes, but he blinked so quickly he left Kad no time for reassurance. "My baby girl died when she was just twenty-one."

Kad sat completely up, his eyes widened in awe. "Shit, big homie, my bad. I didn't mean——"

Zip cut him off. "Little did I know, she had been sneaking around with this li'l nigga that thought he was a gangsta. He stayed way on the opposite side of town." Zip paused and shook his head. It looked like he wanted to break down right there in the entryway. "I received a call from a homicide detective at four a.m. one morning. The car was found riddled with bullets. They both were pronounced dead."

Kad was lost for words.

Zip lowered his head and applied minimal pressure against his lids, seemingly to keep the tears from falling. "I found out later the cat owed someone some paper." Zip chuckled. The tears descended and he let them. "Kad…" He paused. "He only owed dude 20 Gs. If I had been more of a father instead of trying to control her life, she would have come to me for help. I could've gave the youngsta the money and my baby girl would still be here." He used the collar of his shirt to dry his face. "She's going to date. She's going to have sex. That's reality, especially in this day. Time to meet dude, find out what type of guy he is, get involved, pretend to be okay with it so she won't keep nothing from you. No parent should have to bury their child."

"Everyone to the dayroom now!"

Zip peered back at the C.O.s swarming in. Panicky, he spewed, "Youngsta, flush that shit!"

Kad flew off the bunk and rummaged through his things.

"Keep watch," he blurted. His hand trembled as his eyes moved hastily in an attempt to locate the syrup.

Zip discreetly watched the men out the corner of his eyes. He figured they'd be busy regulating the other inmates, which would buy Kad some time.

However, he was wrong. In the process of giving orders, they never slowed their stride. They had a target, and the target was them.

"Hold on, hold them off, Zip!" His words were choppy as his heart raced.

CHAPTER 22
JEWEL

Jewel sat amongst her classmates inside of the massive auditorium. Jewel was swelling with joy like she had just won the lotto. However, what she really won was her man back.

"Oooh, I'm super late, I'm sorry!" Kesha rushed to find the first empty seat in the row.

Jewel had to do a double take. Kesha looked breathtaking. Her long jet-black bundles enhanced her smooth complexion, highlighting her perfectly-beat face. Little did Jewel know that Kesha inwardly felt the same exact way. Plus, Kesha was a bit intimidated knowing that Jewel was fucking her man.

The ceremony began shortly. You would've thought people were there to see Megan, as packed as it was for the thirteen graduates. Jewel glanced and winked at Bobby. She felt like the luckiest woman alive, which came to a sudden halt once she spotted Blotchy a few rows behind her. Jewel's smile faded instantly.

What the hell is he doing here?

Jewel lowered her head as she tried to think of a reason to justify the blatant disrespect. Bobby, on the other hand, turned around in his seat to see what exactly soured Jewel's mood. Immediately, he spotted Blotchy. He appeared to be trying to get Jewel's attention, yet she appeared to be in deep thought. Bobby gritted his teeth, allowing his mind to run away from him.

Don't look, Jewel, don't look, she repeated mentally to keep her life from falling apart in the midst of the ceremony. She and Blotchy had talked about the graduation days prior, with him making an agreement to not show, but chill afterwards. However, he had broken the deal.

Jewel was so busy pondering that she didn't even hear her name being called. A nudge from a middle-aged Hispanic woman snapped her out of her trance. Jewel appeared stunned, peering at the lady through wide eyes.

"Mija." She nodded and pointed towards the stage.

Jewel's teacher was front and center clutching her certificate. "Jewel McVale," she repeated.

Jewel adjusted her cap sheepishly as she stood to her feet. She smoothed the wrinkles from her dress, then peered back at Kesha.

She knows.

The glare in Kesha's eyes conveyed so much anger that it made Jewel's legs buckle. She sighed deeply, straightened her back, and pressed on.

Oh well, that's been my nigga.

Jewel slowly pranced up the stairs, tossing her hair over her shoulder.

Bitch, I'm doing this for my momma. I love you, Danielle.

The thought of her mother gave her the boost of confidence she needed. She was a step closer to becoming an oncologist. She would save as many women as she could to prevent them from losing their lives to the deadly disease. If only someone as passionate could've saved her mother. A single tear slid down her cheek in the midst of grabbing her ribboned certificate. She smiled at her teacher gracefully and wiped the tear away. Jewel took a seat in one of the chairs that was neatly lined up onstage. Squinting past the light, she managed to lock eyes with Bobby, who was still cheering. She waved and smiled. Swiftly, she glanced at Blotchy, who appeared upset. He stared at her menacingly. There wasn't a speck of humor in his eyes. Jewel looked away, not wanting to alert Bobby of any funny business. She had lied to both men about each other, and although it complicated her life greatly, she wasn't ready to expose the truth. She felt a light tap on her knee.

"The graduating class of 2022!"

Oblivious, Jewel jumped to her feet, immediately coming to the realization of what was occurring. In a group, the women exited the stage.

"Are you okay, sweetie?" the Hispanic woman she had been seated by asked.

Jewel sighed deeply. "I'm fine." She shot her a tight-lipped smile. Her brows dipped in confusion.

"You sure? You seem a little distant?"

Jewel could see Bobby marching towards her. "Positive, thanks for your concern." Jewel gave the lady a one-armed hug and headed towards Bobby.

"What's he doing here?" Bobby asked.

Jewel was going to play dumb, but cleared her throat instead. Blotchy was approaching. The hair on her arms rose. She tried to mentally prepare herself for the drama.

"Congratulations," Blotchy announced.

Jewel tensed up, but calmed as she noticed Blotchy looking past her. He cut his eyes in her direction, mugged her as he bypassed, then quickly changed his expression as he greeted his cousin. Kesha stood frozen a few feet behind Jewel. Her smile was tight-lipped as she tried pretending to be as excited as everyone else.

"Oh, okay, I thought it was some fuck shit going on," he spoke loud enough for Blotchy to hear.

Jewel crossed her fingers, hoping Blotchy would remain quiet.

"Come on," he continued, leading the way, placing his hand on her lower back.

"Hey Bobby!" Kesha yelled from behind.

Jewel stopped and turned around, waiting to see what transpired between the two. However, Bobby jerked her by the arm, leading the way, then chucked the deuce at Kesha with his other hand. If Blotchy wouldn't have been standing there with her, Jewel would've definitely turned around and teased her.

As soon as the doors were closed, Bobby turned and faced Jewel.

"I did have other plans tonight, but I'm going to just reschedule it until your birthday."

Jewel's brows dipped. She was appalled. She couldn't fathom why he was so upset. Things could've easily gotten real ugly.

"But why?"

"Something tells me you not right, Jewel. I'm not stupid, and I know y'all are still seeing each other."

Jewel threw her hands up. "Oh my God, you're so crazy!"

"That's what your mouth is saying. You know the real."

Unfortunately, she did. The shit was eating her up and she was growing tired of the lies and deceit.

Shortly, he parked in front of the house.

"I'm going to holla at Dooski and see if he is down to record. I'll be back in a few. Text me if you need something."

Jewel climbed out of the Escalade without parting her lips. She was back at square one. She dragged inside, inwardly hoping Bobby would change his mind and turn around. She stepped inside and locked the door behind her. She tossed the keys on the table then removed her heels.

KNOCK! KNOCK! KNOCK!

I knew he would change his mind.

A smile slowly crept onto her face as she opened the door.

"Blotchy?"

"I don't say shit to you at the ceremony. Like a sucka, I played my role. This is my time now, right?" His question sounded more like a demand as he eyed her like a neglected child would his mother.

Being in Blotchy's presence was always so relaxed and delightful, but after what he just witnessed at the ceremony, she knew it would be everything but that. She knew there was no denying Bobby after tonight. She needed to tell him the truth.

She gathered her things and left, texting Bobby in the process.

Jewel: I'm with Myesha. I'll be home later.

CHAPTER 23
MYESHA

"Hands on ya knees, bitch, buss it back (aye)
Through the tights you can see this pussy fat (aye)
Through the them pockets I can see a nigga racks (aye)
I'm a money making' bitch, no cap (aye)..."

Megan Thee Stallion blared through the massive speakers inside of the crowded strip club. Two brown-skinned baddies who appeared to be twins were on stage.

Ooooh, them hoes bad.

She peered behind her and spotted Bianca, who was still standing by the door talking to the bouncer. Bianca had major clout inside of the clubs and Myesha witnessed it with her own eyes. This was the third club they had been to within an hour, looking for Brandi. Myesha had tried her to talk Bianca out of pulling up, but she shut her down. She figured she'd chill and enjoy the show, since Bianca was preoccupied. She snapped her fingers and sang along to the lyrics, dropping her head. Slowly she lifted it, spotting Bianca marching towards the rear of the club. She took off behind her. She was moving quickly, but secretly, trying not to draw any attention. The door to the dressing room was slightly ajar once Myesha bent the corner.

Myesha slid inside and closed the door behind her. She watched Bianca stomp down the hall, peering left to right. A few women lingered inside. Some were wondering what was occurring and others glanced in her direction and finished preparing to go onstage. Slowly, Myesha followed her.

"I'm not going to even sneak. You put ya shit down and run that shit," Bianca said, stepping backwards. She didn't have to remove a piece of clothing or jewelry. She had already done so in the car. Dressed in a black and white Adidas sports bra with matching tights and shell toes, she was ready.

Myesha's heart beat fast and her steps quickened. The locker blocked Brandi from the angle she was coming from, but as she hurried closer, her deceitful sister came into view.

Brandi chuckled. "Oh, this what this about?" She pointed at Myesha while slowly removing her jewelry.

"You got two seconds or I'm gonna drag you with all of that shit on. I didn't come here to talk. If that's the case, I would've called."

Someone yelled from the rear of the dressing room, and their heads swiveled in the direction. Footsteps approaching forced Myesha and Bianca to turn back around. It was Brandi running up on Bianca. Bianca had spotted her in the nick of time. Brandi swung wildly as soon as she was within reach. Bianca, who was two inches taller with a longer reach, stood back and went to work. She threw two straight jabs, snapping Brandi's head backwards. Brandi shook it off and dipped low, hooking Bianca in the stomach. She winced a little, but swiftly brought her knee up, connecting with Brandi's jaw, causing her to stumble back. She felt her lip and indeed, there was blood. Feeling played, Brandi rushed her again. One punch grazed her chin and a few of them bounced off Bianca's arm.

A right uppercut sent Brandi stumbling backwards, only this time, Bianca didn't let up.

BAM! BAM! BAM! BAM!

After every jab she inched forward, walking Brandi all the way to the door they had come in. The last punch put her on her ass. Before her body dropped, Bianca was already kicking. She kicked her in her shins and thighs until she was flat on her back. She kicked her with force in her midsection, and instead of cocking back her foot, she lifted it.

BOOM! She paused.

BOOM! Blood spewed from Brandi's nose and mouth on impact.

BOOM! Her head bounced off the concrete.

"Okay, Bianca, okay, you gon' kill her!" Myesha yelled hysterically. She was the only onlooker who seemed bothered.

Truthfully, Brandi had a galore of enemies. She was cutthroat and grimy. Everywhere she went, she got over, even if it was for a little of nothing. It was merely something she just had to do.

BOOM! Bianca kicked her one last time before backing way.

"The fuck y'all looking at?" Bianca screamed.

The girls who had been looking scurried like a bunch of ants. She bent down beside Brandi before leaving.

"I'm taking ya bread. This the dough you should have bonded her out with." She paused, sneering in disgust. "Whenever you want it back or want to do some punching, you know where I'm at, bitch. I should go kick ya momma's ass too, but I'm gon give her a pass 'cause she old." Bianca stood to leave, giving Brandi one last glare. "Come on, sis."

Myesha followed closely behind.

The car was silent as they drove. Myesha had no idea where to.

"Look, sis." She paused, peering straight ahead. She hadn't bothered to wipe the blood from the knuckles as she gripped the steering wheel tighter. "I know you love Momma. It's natural. I hate to admit it, but I love her too."

Myesha nodded.

"Just whatever you do, never trust her." She lifted her index finger from the steering wheel, wagging it from left to right. "She's stuck in her ways and she been who she is for a very long time. Change is simply not in her plans. Love her from a distance."

"Okay," Myesha responded, then lowered her head.

Bianca stopped at the light, then faced her. "I'm serious. Stay away from Momma." She pointed.

Myesha nodded.

"Secondly, I can tell you love dude. I'm not gon' hold you hostage. I was a fool before once, maybe twice. If you want to go back to your little apartment, I'll take you."

Myesha smiled.

"I'll take that as a yes. Where am I going?"

Twenty minutes later, Bianca was parked outside of Dooski apartment. "Call me if you need me."

"Okay, thanks sis. I love you." Myesha opened the door.

"Hold on. Here." She reached into the back seat and handed Myesha the Crown Royal bag.

Myesha's brows dipped in confusion as she peered from the bag back to Bianca. "Why are you giving me this?"

"Girl, get this. I just took it 'cause she didn't deserve it. You just got out. Go buy yourself something nice." Bianca smiled.

Myesha hugged Bianca. "Thanks again," she said before climbing out of the Charger.

Bianca waited until the door opened to drive off.

Myesha stood there as she and Dooski locked eyes. Both of them conveyed each other's agony, but neither of them was able to voice it, as badly as both of them wanted to act out in aggression. Audacity and excitement predominated the anger once they stood near each other for the first time in weeks. Everything they mentally planned went completely out of the window until images of the woman he cherished being with another man arose.

"I, um, just got out," Myesha said in a low tone.

"Why you didn't go over that nigga house you took the charge for?"

Offended, Myesha scowled. "Nigga?" she asked, her face contorted in bewilderment.

"Yeah. Brandi told me you was in the car with some nigga and the laws rolled y'all."

Her mouth dropped and her eyes widened in shock. *I'm glad Bianca whooped her ass.* Myesha smirked and shook her head. "Wow, is that what she told you?" She peered at him through slits.

Dooski stared back at her unblinkingly.

Hot tears streamed down her face "I was in the car with her! She told me she already had two pending drug charges and if I took it, she would bond me out! She lied! Bianca bonded me out and we just left the club from whooping her ass. My psychotic mother put her up to it!" she explained hysterically, her face soiled with the salty liquid that fell freely from her eyes.

Dooski stepped back, overwhelmed and appalled by all the information. He couldn't believe he allowed another bitch to sway him into turning on the only woman who had his heart. He reached out and pulled her into his chest. "Baby girl, I'm sorry, I'm so sorry. Please forgive me," he begged.

"Aye, Dooski, you good?" Bobby asked, standing behind him in the doorway. "Myesha?" He scowled, inching closer to ensure that his eyes wasn't fooling him.

"Huh?" she answered, lifting her head from Dooski's chest.

Bobby's eyes widened. "What's going on? Where is Jewel?"

Both Dooski's and Myesha's brows dipped. They were certainly dumbfounded.

Myesha shrugged. "I don't know, Bobby, I just got out."

As soon as the words spewed from her mouth, she regretted it, knowing the type of time her cousin was on.

Ah'Million

CHAPTER 24
KAD

Kad had counted the lines on the bricks a hundred times. There was no clock or even a window for him to even attempt to count the days he had spent inside of the segregation cell. It felt like it was weeks ago when they tossed him inside of the cell. No property whatsoever. Not a bible or a roll of tissue. He was simply out of luck if he had to take a shit. He reeked of must, mildew, and ass. The only thing that kept him sane was prayer and exercise. He would do burpees and push-ups until he was drenched in sweat. He sat on the bunk with his knees to his chest and his head buried in his knees.

Hearing the locks click, he spun around towards the door.

"McVale, get dressed and step out."

"I am dressed!" Kad shot back, standing to his feet. He moved towards the door. He squeezed his eyes shut, raising his hand to block out the bright light that irritated his eyes once the cell's doors opened. "Where are we going?" Kad mumbled, not wanting to speak any louder, afraid of the smell that might emerge.

The C.O. calmly ignored him.

Kad shook his head. He was fuming on the inside. He hadn't dealt with that amount of disrespect when he was broke, and everyone knows no one respects you when you're broke. Not even your kids. That's why he always attained the get up and go mentality, to avoid being handled like a peon.

Kad thought his eyes were playing tricks on him when he spotted Loc coming out of Lieutenant Mayes's office.

The fuck he doing?

Kad scowled as they locked eyes, bypassing each other down the long hallway. Loc nodded and proceeded. It was the same nod Zip had given him the day they were thrown into the cell.

"I got it from here, Yarbrough," she spoke, seated behind her desk, looking at the papers that were seen on top.

"Ten-four."

Kad watched the C.O. leave, then awaited instructions. Lieutenant Mayes was feisty. The last thing he wanted to hear was her mouth. Then again, she was so fucking sexy, so hearing her bitch didn't sound like a bad idea after all. A smile etched his face upon thinking about it.

She lifted her head. "Mr. McVale, you——" Her face contorted in confusion. "What the hell are you smiling about?" She rose to her feet, planting both palms on the desk. "You think it's a game where you smuggle drugs inside of my place of employment? Huh?" she continued, daring him to agree.

"Can I be honest?" Kad took one step closer. He had been trying to impress her since he laid eyes on her and he would be damned if he let his stank breath and funky ass fuck up his shot.

"I sure as hell don't want to know any lies." She crossed her arms over her chest, poking out her lips.

Damn, this bitch sexy. Kad grinned. "Mayes, you sexy as fuck. You'd make a blind man smile."

"You got game. Sit down, McVale."

"Cool!" Kad eased onto the chair, careful not to flop.

"McVale, what did you do with the lean?"

"Lean?" Kad's brows dipped in confusion.

"You know what the hell I'm talking about. Syrup, purp, drank, hell, Waukesha, whatever you want to call it."

Kad chuckled. "So you with the shits?"

"McVale, I know what you here for. You already in some deep shit."

"These females lied on me 'cause they after my paper, baby. You seen how they did old man Cosby." Kad crossed his feet and leaned back. "If you ask me about it, that means you don't have it. Right?" he continued.

"I was just seeing if you were going to give me some additional information. The investigation ended yesterday when your boy spoke up and claimed the shit that didn't make it down the toilet,"

Damn, all that shit didn't make it down? That's why I been in this motherfucka for so long.

Lieutenant Mayes stood and walked around her desk, slightly leaning against it. Kad peered at her through curious eyes.

"McVale, I know the shit probably was yours."

"Wait, Zip said it was his?" Kad's brow raised.

Mayes nodded her head.

Kad reclined in his seat, awestruck. That was the last thing he was expecting to hear. *But why is she telling me about this?* He sighed. "Why are you telling me this?" he asked.

"You a cool li'l dude, McVale, with pure intents. I mean, the investigation is over with. I can talk about it all I want now and even though I never really liked Zip 'cause he was disrespectful, after owning that shit, I see him differently. I know those charges are bullshit and I can tell what you are about by the way you move. He still a fuck nigga though. But fuck all of that. You don't need to be in no extra shit anyways. I need you out here so I can see what you really about."

Kad grinned, putting his fist up to his mouth in an attempt to conceal his excitement. He rubbed his hands together. "Say less."

"There was an informant though. He wrote a statement on you and Jackson."

"Who?"

"Daniels."

"Boy Boy?" Kad questioned. His face twisted like he had eaten something sour. "Wow," Kad mouthed, stunned. He was so appalled it was funny. A week prior, he had looked out for Boy Boy and blessed him with an ounce, seeing how rough shit had gotten for him since they snatched his medication.

"He probably mad because y'all was stepping on his toes," she voiced.

"Let that be the reason. So the investigation over, right?"

"You were never a part of it. I just had to make shit look good." She winked.

"So can I rap with Zip real quick?"

Mayes crossed her arms over her chest.

"I guess I'll give you five minutes once I take you to gather your things."

Kad grinned. "Shit, I don't have nothing to gather, but we can take a detour."

"Come on."

Mayes and Kad kept the conversation minimal as he walked on the segregated hallway. "Just go in and come out when I open the door," she stated, unlocking Zip's cell door.

Zip thought that he was seeing a ghost when Kad stepped in.

"Big homie, I just want to tell ya I 'preciate you for keeping your word and you gonna hear from me as soon as I get out."

Zip cracked a smile. He knew Kad would witness the real one day. He knew the youngsta didn't trust him and partially, he couldn't blame him.

"Look, Kad, I want to tell you something before you go." Zip ran his hand over his face. "That day I had that visit, it was Blotchy. He did mention your name, but I wasn't even on that type of time he was on, so he changed the topic "

I knew it.

"What you mean he mentioned my name, and why you just now telling me?"

"It's irrelevant. It's possible that blood would've been shed." he paused. "I deaded that shit. I handled it." He patted his chest.

Kad nodded.

"I just wanted to you to hear the truth from me instead of half of the truth from one of them fuck niggas in the dorm."

"Bet. I'm gon' take ya word for it," Kad responded, jabbing the air with his finger in Zip's direction. He grinned and stood to his feet, and the two men embraced.

The sound of keys jingling indicated their time was up.

"A'ight, boy."

CHAPTER 25
BLOTCHY

"Bae, where we going?" Jewel inquired innocently. She knew she was in deep shit. Blotchy hadn't spoken one word since the doors on his car slammed shut. "Blotchy?" she begged as she turned to face him. "Please say something," Jewel continued.

"When were you going to tell me?" he asked.

Her heart raced suddenly as she spotted the muscle in his temple move. She sighed deeply, unsure of what to say.

Blotchy struck the dash. "When the fuck you was gon' tell me, bruh!" A tear slid down Blotchy's cheek as his chest rose and fell.

Pain pervaded through her immediately. Although Blotchy had hurt her deeply once before. it dismantled her spirit to witness his pain now.

Blotchy recklessly swerved into the lot of the bootleg Chinese place. Once coming to a complete stop, he turned and faced her. "Don't lie to me either. Jewel." he spoke through clenched teeth.

His eyes were filled with agony and his voice was choppy. There was no way she could add to the pain. He verbally begged for the truth, but his glare simply yearned for mercy. She hurt him, which meant she was the only one that could heal him, and if a simple lie could mend the pain, then so be it. However, the truth was evident.

"That's that nigga baby, isn't it?" He glared.

The fluttering in her chest was so immense she thought she would have a heart attack. "Is it my turn to speak now?" Jewel asked to buy herself more time.

Blotchy relaxed his grip on the steering wheel and reclined in his seat. "Do ya thang," he said, staring straight ahead.

"Truth is, Blotchy, I haven't had sex since the day we made love in your studio," she lied.

Blotchy's head slowly swiveled in her direction.

"When you beat me like that, I almost lost my baby, so I made a vow to myself that I'd keep you from him or her."

A slow smile etched his face. "You crazy. You ain't keeping me from my motherfucking seed!" he screamed, joyfully reaching over his seat wrapping her up in his arms tightly.

"Move, bae!" Jewel joked playfully. Jewel sighed deeply.

"Bae, I know I tripped out and that shit was foul." He paused. "But, um…that's why I been going out of my way to show you just how sorry I am, and prove to you that I'm not a sorry motherfucker. I just made a terrible decision."

Gently, he grabbed her by the chin and pulled her in for a kiss. Slowly, their lips merged. They closed their eyes while savoring such intimacy. Jewel pulled back.

"I was going to surprise you, bae," she whispered, mere inches from his face.

Blotchy relaxed his grip, slowly easing back to his side. He cleared his throat. "Jewel," Blotchy whispered, yet she heard him clearly as if he was yelling. "You are the best thing that has happened to me in a long time. I've had success with the music shit, made enough money for the both of us. As far as a surprise, I'm not too familiar with that term. Never really knew what a surprise was because as a kid, we never celebrated holidays or birthdays." He lowered his head. "You would've thought my mother was a Jehovah's Witness or something. Nah." He paused, shaking his head. "Truth is, we were just broke as fuck."

A tear slid down Jewel's face. She reached over and wrapped her arms around his neck. "Aww, baby, I'm sorry."

Blotchy cracked a smile. "It's cool, mama. As long as I got you and my seed, I'm good. On God."

Jewel nodded. The tears fell in abundance. It cut her deeply to steady inflict so much pain on a man who was enduring and had been through so much agony. She knew her promises were void as a hot check. Nothing she uttered was guaranteed. She wished she could simply walk away from Bobby and live happily ever after with Blotchy, but shit wasn't that simple.

"Bae, look, now that we 'bout to have this baby, I have to get back on with the label," he said, knowing that he had already been replaced. "Have you spoken with your pops yet?"

"No, um, he hasn't called yet," Jewel lied again.

"Okay, okay." He appeared to be in deep thought. He turned to face her. "You know, if I take Dooski out of the picture, they'll have no choice but to sign me."

Jewel's eyes narrowed as she peered at him in disbelief. "What the hell are you implying?" Jewel's brows dipped as the pace of her heart increased.

Blotchy grinned. "I'm fucking with you, bae." *No the fuck I'm not. If that's what I have to do, then so be it.* "Let's go order this food, bae."

Blotchy opened the car door and Jewel followed suit. Hand in hand, they walked inside of the small establishment. It was Jewel's favorite Chinese place. Jewel and Blotchy chatted aimlessly as they walked out of the restaurant and to his car.

A truck veered hastily into the lot, stopping a few inches away from them.

"Who the fuck?" Blotchy blurted, halting mid-stride. His hand moved to the handle on his F&N. The truck abruptly stopped, forcing it to jerk forward. The door flung open.

It was Bobby.

Blotchy sighed and took his hand off his tool.

"So you lied to me? Bobby yelled. He was certainly enraged. "You been lying!" he continued, marching towards them.

She had desperately wanted to come clean, but she was waiting for the perfect opportunity. This time, she would have to tell the truth, whether she wanted to or not. Things had definitely gotten out of hand.

Ah'Million

CHAPTER 26
JEWEL

Panicky, Jewel peered swiftly from Bobby to Blotchy. Her hands shook uncontrollably as she begin to choke on her tears. Bobby's behavior was erratic. It surely wasn't one of an "uncle"

"Oh, you can't talk?" Bobby inched closer.

I knew this shit would happen just like this.

"Hey, just chill," Blotchy spoke, lifting his arm in an attempt to keep space between the two.

"Bruh, don't talk to me." Bobby pulled up his jeans, shifting his focus from Jewel to Blotchy.

Skkrr!

A black Tahoe veered into the lot. The three of them squinted to see past the tint. Bobby pulled his gun from the waist of his jeans, but the men were a lot quicker.

BOOM! BOOM! BOOM! BOOM!

Blotchy pushed Jewel to the ground. Bobby dived on top of her. The two of them being low made Blotchy an easy target. His body jerked left to right as he ate the bullets. He stammered like a drunk. Blood oozed from every hole. His face contorted in pain as he winced, trying to breathe to suppress the burning sensation.

BOOM!

A final shot between his eyes dropped him like a sack of potatoes. He was dead before he hit the cement. They pulled off.

Jewel sobbed beneath Bobby's body. Slowly, Bobby rolled to the side, seeing the gunmen were gone. Jewel scurried to her knees. Bobby winced as he grabbed his leg. A palm-sized bloodstain decorated his jeans.

"Oh my God!" Panicky, Jewel shook uncontrollably, afraid of what to do next. From the corner of her eye, she saw Blotchy laying on top of the pavement motionless.

"Oh no!" she wailed. She hurried to her feet and rushed over to him. "Blotchy, no!" she whispered as tears streamed down her cheeks. She clung on to his clothes as if she could pull him back to life. "Blotchy!" she hollered hysterically. She shook him. "Wake up!" She buried her head on top of his.

He was already cold. His eyes were vacant and his lips were curled into a smirk.

She planted a kiss on his forehead, then wailed louder. "Why?" She lifted his head and gently placed it onto her lap as she rocked slowly back and forth. She shook her head sympathetically. *He didn't deserve this.*

"Jewel." Bobby's voice was raspy but audible as he squirmed a bit.

"Huh?" she voiced, snapping out of her trance. Seeing Blotchy's lifeless body had completely distracted her from tending to Bobby.

A nasty cough fell from his lips. Jewel gently placed Blotchy's head on the concrete and ran over to Bobby.

"Help me up," he whispered.

Their hands intertwined as Jewel used all of her strength to help Bobby to his feet. The sharp pain forced him to yelp in distress as he limped forward. Jewel stood still.

"What about Blotchy?" she inquired.

Bobby stiffened, then turned around to face Jewel. "What you mean?" He mugged her. "We gon' leave his ass right here!" He jabbed his finger downward.

Jewel's mouth fell open. Grief crammed her bedroom eyes as tears immediately threatened to fall. "I-I..." she stammered. The weight of the agony ceased her speech. *His life matters too, dead or alive. I just can't leave him out here. He wouldn't do that to me.* Jewel caressed her arm. "I'm going to wait here with him until the police come." Her words dripped with apprehension. However, she was going to make sure he was properly tended to and not just left sprawled out on the pavement like a piece of trash.

"Really?" Bobby grunted. He breathlessly planted his body against his truck. His veins protruded as he tightly gripped his wound. "Look at me, Jewel." His chest rose and fell. A permanent mug etched his face. "You gon' really make me drive myself? You love this nigga?" He inhaled and exhaled sharp and quickly.

He's hurting. He needs me.

Overwhelmed, Jewel simply didn't know what to do. There was no way Bobby could successfully drive himself, yet there was no way she was going to leave Blotchy. She swiftly removed her phone from her bra.

"Dooski!" she yelled into the receiver.

"Yeah, yeah, what's up?"

"Some dudes just shot at us. Blotchy is dead and Bobby is shot. I have to get him to a hospital. Can you please get here now so that you can make sure h-he's not just out here like this!" Jewel swallowed the lump in her throat along with salty tears. She had never felt such devastation.

"Take Bobby to the hospital now. I'll meet up with y'all afterwards."

Ah'Million

CHAPTER 27
3 MONTHS LATER
KAD

Kad and his attorney, Myron Stouter, sat inside of a small room, prepping for court. Today was the third day of trial and Kad hoped it would be his last. His court date had been postponed numerous times due to the possible absence of his D.A.

"Look, you know the prosecutor wants your ass."

Kad's prosecutor had been hospitalized during the time of his first court date. He managed to postpone the date of his trial until he was released from the hospital. Kad nodded his head, attentively listening to his attorney. He was afraid. He didn't want to voice it, but inwardly, he felt as frightened as he did when he was a child and his mother would leave him alone at home for days at a time before returning.

Mr. Strouter leaned against the corner of the table with his arms crossed at his chest. "Mr. McVale, you good?" he asked.

Mr. Stouter wasn't the typical attorney. He was born and raised in slums. He sold, stole, and even used drugs once upon a time in his life. His mother died when he was four. His dad raised him. When he was fifteen, his father died in front of him. A police officer shot and killed him. Shortly after, Stouter developed a burning desire to pursue law, since the officer only received a puny three-year sentence. He figured he'd avenge his father's death by helping prosecute men of authority by representing those seeking justice.

"I'm good, man," Kad voiced, massaging his kneecaps.

Stouter gave Kad a pat on his back. "Let's do this then."

Sierra bounced in her seat and she smiled wickedly at Kad as he made his way down the aisle of the courtroom. Kad paid her no mind whatsoever. If it hadn't been for the absence of Bobby and Jewel, he wouldn't have been surveying the room in the first place.

Where are they?

His brows crimped. He found their absence quite odd. However, for the first time since the trial began, he spotted Susie. His stomach started doing somersaults. He swallowed the lump in his throat, confused by her presence.

Perhaps something went wrong and that's the reason behind Bobby's absence, he thought. *Chill, Bobby handled that. But why isn't he here?* Kad's stomach bubbled up. He squeezed his cheeks tight to avoid shitting himself.

Shortly after, court began. The prosecutor called Susie to the stand. Kad cursed under his breath as soon as he locked eyes with her.

That stupid-ass lipstick.

It was that lipstick that fueled his fire, that crimson red that had covered his dick, staining it in the process. That same lipstick made him bend her over his wooden desk, and that's why he sat in the courtroom today.

"Ms. Mackin, tell us again what happened on March 8, 2022?"

"Whatever it says is what happened."

The prosecutor blinked rapidly, appalled by her remark.

"Um, Mrs. Mackin, how about you begin with a vivid description of the setting on March 8th?"

"How imperative is it?"

"Well, Ms. Mackin, it's very imperative. The situation is detrimental for both parties - yours especially."

The fuck that s'posed to mean? If the bitch lies on me, that shit is serious as well.

An awkward silence filled the room.

This is it.

She was going to either ride with Bobby or roll on him.

She rolled her eyes impatiently, then lowered her head. Slowly, she lifted it, shaking it. "Fine, yes, we had sex." Aggression laced her words.

"Did he force you, Ms. Mackin?" He placed his hand in his pocket.

"No, it was consensual, and if the chance presents itself, I'll do it again."

The entire courtroom gasped. Kad's eyes widened in shock.

"He made her say that! He's a monster!" Sierra blurted hysterically.

Judge Davoy banged the gavel. "Order in the court!" the judge yelled. "Mr. Thomas, anything else?"

The prosecutor looked at Susie, then at Kad, and back to the judge before saying, "No sir."

"This case is being dismissed for inappropriate conduct. Evidence fails to show that Ms. Mackin's accusation can be proved beyond a reasonable doubt."

The courtroom erupted in chaos instead of satisfaction. Susie stepped down the stairs and down the long aisle. Her husband leaped from his seat and followed behind her.

"Really? You lied to me, you cheated on me with…with this?"

She stopped and turned around. "With what? A black guy? Yes, hell the fuck yes! And I've come to the realization that I love black dick." She aggressively removed her ring and stuffed it into his shirt pocket. "I'm done faking orgasms. I'm going to live how I want and fuck who I want, 'cause even though you gave me everything, I still wasn't happy, and as long as I'm with you, I'll never be." Susie spun on her heels and headed out of the door.

Her husband looked like a man who had been stood up by his bride on his wedding day.

Screams erupted from the other side of the door. Everyone stopped moving, trying to decipher what was occurring. Shortly after, Susie flew back inside of the courtroom as Sierra rained blow after blow.

"I'll kill you, bitch, for fucking with my money."

Blood spewed from Susie's nose as she tried her damndest to defend herself. Her long legs waggled helplessly, but it wasn't enough. Sierra hovered over her, putting all her might in every blow.

The male guard came from behind the door where Kad stood, tackling Sierra to the ground. She wiggled free and darted towards Susie and began whaling on her again. Another officer arrived and they were finally able to restrain her. They cuffed her and lifted her to her feet. She and Kad unintentionally locked eyes as she was being escorted out.

Kad grinned and mumbled, "Deuces."

"Fuck you!" she hollered.

The men forced her out of the room quicker. Kad was elated, knowing that soon she'd get a taste of what it was like on the inside.

CHAPTER 28
DOOSKI

"I'm not in competition with my homies
   I'm whippin the competition and the Rollie
   I know my opposition never knew me
   They wouldn't be opposition the if they know me
   I made a proposition to my hitters.
   I told 'em to knock 'em down if you owe me
   I just been sliding round hitting buildings
   We moving that Glock, pounds and them.40's
   Them niggas got shot down, we was whorin
   My homie a opp now so we on him I was like sixteen with the
MAC on me
   Deep in the field like its Pop Warner
   Weathered the shit scene, niggas cracked on me
   When it got real tried to slide on him
   I made some M's, split the guys on it
   We keeping it real, niggas not
   And my homie a savage got put in a casket
   And I'm mad at him 'cause he died on us
   Just left the viewing and I told his mom
   Every time that she cry, we gon' slide on 'em..."

Dooski bobbed his head to the beat as he swerved in and out of traffic. Today was simply one of those days thoughts and images of Blotchy filled his mind, so he hit the streets alone to mourn his best friend.

Since Blotchy's death, Dooski had been adamant on penalizing the men responsible. He had grown to love Blotchy like a brother. Losing two men he trusted with his life drove him to despair, slowly ebbing his spirit. Vengeance was dire and until the one who killed his blood lay in blood, he wouldn't rest. He roamed the streets morning, noon, and night.

He and Myesha had become inseparable.

Forgiving a fault brings you closer.

Myesha had even given him permission to seduce another woman in exchange for information regarding Blotchy's assailant. She conveyed how crippled he felt not being able to even the score. Whatever made him smile and sleep better, she was for it, and vice versa. Once Dooski found out all of the relevant information, his relations with the chick lessened.

"You better not be giving that bitch none of my dick, Dooski. That's not part of the plan."

Dooski cracked a smile as he recalled Myesha's words. Today was different. He wasn't on the lurk. He finally had the drop on his target and he was trailing him, trying to decide the perfect time to make his move.

Ring! Ring! Ring!

"Hello?" Dooski answered.

"Bae, me and my momma on our way to the hospital. Jewel is in labor!"

"Okay, I'll meet you up there." Dooski scowled. "Did you say you were with your momma?"

"Yes, and bae, so much has happened. I have so much to tell you, so hurry up."

"Wai-wait, Myesha, I'm——"

"Just hurry up and get here."

Myesha ended the call and Dooski ended his mission…for the moment.

CHAPTER 29
BOBBY

"Aaarrgghh!" Jewel howled as Bobby and the male nurse helped her from the wheelchair to her bed.

Bobby chuckled softly. "Girl, the process hasn't even started yet."

She turned around and rolled her eyes at Bobby. Gradually, they were progressing, but Bobby was still the same ol' Bobby.

"Get on that damn bed." He pointed. "With all that ass hanging out."

Jewel smacked her lips, then grinned before slowly easing onto the bed. "Ugh!" She reclined, a bit relieved.

Bobby leaned down and planted a soft kiss on her forehead. "I'm 'bout to step out real quick and call my granny. Just holla if you need me."

Bobby rushed out of the room and into the hallway, praying his phone would work. "Hey Granny," Bobby said, closing the door to Jewel's room.

"Hey baby!"

"She about to have the baby, Granny." A smile etched Bobby's face. At the moment, he probably wouldn't admit it, but Bobby was anxious as a child on the night before Christmas. He couldn't wait to hold, love, and nurture his seed. Secretly, he had longed for a family since losing his mother and father.

Bobby's grandmother gasped sharply. "What?" He had caught her off guard. "Why didn't you come and get me? Bobby, please come and get your granny. I've been waiting on this moment forever."

Bobby grinned, shaking his head slowly. "I got you, Granny. Get dressed. I'm on my way." Bobby turned around to head back inside.

"Bobby!"

He squinted down the hall. Myesha and another chick were headed in his direction.

"Where is my boy at?" he asked as soon as Myesha was in ear-shot.

She placed a hand over her chest. "Whew! I'm tired," she said, breathing heavily. "He is on his way." She paused, giving him a hug from the side. "How is she?"

"She being a big baby." He put his hand on the knob. "Bey?" His brows dipped, awestruck and appalled all at once.

"How are you, Bobby?" She flashed a tight-lipped smile.

Myesha lowered her head, placing her hair behind her ears.

Bobby was never really fond of Bey, but she was family. He loved her just as much as Kad loved her. Bey's appearance had changed drastically. It looked as if she had lost thirty to forty pounds since the last time she saw her. You could tell it wasn't a healthy weight loss which consisted of working out and eating right. Everything sagged, including the bags under her eyes.

"I'm straight. Are you straight, is the question?"

"I have just been going through it, but I'm good." She nodded.

Damn, she even lost a few teeth.

Tears brimmed in her eyes.

"It got that bad, B?" Bobby squinted in utter disbelief. "Myesha, go check on Jewel. Let me holla at your moms."

Myesha nodded and went inside.

Bobby grabbed Bey by the shoulders and before he could utter a word, Bey leaned in, burying her head into his chest. She sobbed uncontrollably. It was long overdue.

"It's all my fault, Bobby. I haven't been able to live with myself. I fucked over everyone I love."

"It's all right, Bey, calm down." He patted her on the back.

She pulled back. "Some fool killed my baby! Kad found out that I lied to get his money!" She jabbed her chest with her index finger. "He gave me that money to hire a lawyer." She paused. "He had already been dead a week when I got that money from Kad! I knew he was dead!" Tears fell in an abundance, soaking her face. "For days, I plotted against my own child" She beat her chest like it was a drum. "I wanted vengeance. I was so busy highlighting the way they lived instead of showing them the right way. Look at

Brandi. She's dead," she rambled on, her bottom lip trembling. "She's dead." Her high-pitched voice faded off into a whisper.

"Who, Bey? Who? Who's dead?" Bobby asked through widened eyes.

"They found Brandi in the trunk of a car last night dead." She sniffled, using her hand to erase the tears. "She had multiple stab wounds. The side of her face was bashed in. They found her ID in her bra and stopped by the house and I had to go identify her. The hardest shit I ever done."

"Aww, man." Bobby pulled her in tighter.

Bey wailed like a newborn child and by the time she was done, his T-shirt was soaked.

"Let go of that guilt, Bey. Love her through Myesha and Bianca and just ask God for forgiveness. Come on."

Bey and Bobby stepped inside

"Jewel, I'm about to go get this granny of mine. She says it's a must she be here." Bobby smiled as he exaggerated at the end of his statement.

"O-Okay," Jewel said, practicing her breathing. She looked like she was in pain.

Bobby and Bey locked eyes briefly before he made his way out of the room and hospital. He rushed down the hallway and out of the exit. He removed his phone out of his pocket, scrolling through his contacts, A strong gust of wind lifted the bottom of his shirt. He peered up ahead at the car that sped past him.

What the fuck? He squinted to get a closer look. *Kesha? The fuck?* He would have missed her if he hadn't looked up when he did. *What is she doing here?* He didn't have the time to attempt to figure it out.

He rushed to his truck and headed to his grandmother's.

He vowed to give Jewel whatever her heart desired on her birthday, and her request was to spend the day with him and to meet the woman he held so close to his heart. His grandmother didn't ask, nor did he volunteer. She was simply elated to be meeting a woman Bobby had dealings with. She fell in love with Jewel instantly.

Bobby sighed deeply. The last person he would have to face and hope for their approval was Kad. It had been almost a year that he and Jewel had been courting and to his knowledge, neither of them had mentioned it to Kad. A huge smile etched Bobby's face, then he chuckled softly. The sight of his grandmother waiting patiently on the porch warmed his heart, and if that didn't, her inviting smile did. He stepped out of his truck and around it. She used her cane to ease up off the ground.

"Hey baby!" She glowed. The way she glowed, you would've thought she was the one about to go into labor. She kissed Bobby on the cheek and he planted one on her forehead as he led her to the truck. He opened her door and helped her inside.

Ring! Ring! Ring!

Bobby's phone sounded in the midst of him climbing inside. It was Myesha. Seeing her name on the screen instantly sent him into panic mode.

"What's up, Myesha?"

"Bobby, Jewel is having this baby. He's coming now!"

The phone fell into Bobby's lap as he pressed down on the pedal. "Hold on, Granny, Jewel having the baby," he voiced, placing his arm a few inches in front of her in case her body jerked forward from his speedy take off

"What?" she asked, stunned.

"Jewel is having the baby."

"Ooohh, baby, hurry up!" She clasped her hands in front of her, placing them in her lap.

The GPS said the drive was twenty-one minutes away. However, Bobby pulled into the lot in fifteen.

"Granny, I know you can't move fast, but I need you to move the fastest you ever moved," he said, slowing against the curb.

She undid her seatbelt. "Chile, you just don't know." Her door was open before the car completely stopped.

Bobby parked and rushed to her side. She was already out of the truck.

"Come on, I'm behind you. Lead the way baby."

Her steps were small, but quick. Bobby peered over his shoulder at her while galloping down the hallway. Eventually, Bobby put distance between them. He didn't try to. He was simply elated and couldn't help it.

"Granny, this the room, number six!" he yelled in front of the door.

Granny had slowed a bit, but she was still moving. Onlookers peered at him in confusion. She waved him off.

"G'wone in there. I'm behind ya." She paused, catching her breath. "I'll catch up."

Bobby rushed inside.

"Push!"

Grunts and moans filled the room as Jewel gave it everything she had. You could tell by the number of veins protruding that she was really stressing and straining. Bobby rushed around the doctors and next to her side.

"You're the father?" the male doctor asked.

"Yeah, that's my seed."

He waved Bobby over. "Come on, give me a hand. His head is at the opening. One more good push and were done."

Bobby gladly assisted the doctor.

"Aaagghh!" Jewel screamed.

"Calm down, chile, it's almost over," Bobby's grandmother voiced, leaning against the wall breathless.

Jewel smiled for a mini-second before pain engulfed her. "Aaagghh!"

"Come on, Jewel, push for me," the doctor urged.

"The fuck?" The sight of the top of the baby's head emerging from Jewel's womb nearly sent Bobby crashing to the floor. Vomit ascended, leaving a foul taste in his mouth.

"You okay?" the doctor peered over his shoulder.

"Mmmmmph!" Jewel pushed, her eyes squeezed shut.

Gently, the doctor pulled slowly.

"Aaaahh!" she howled like an injured wolf.

"I see his shoulders!"

"Come on, Jewel!"

Everyone except Bobby cheered. The sight of it all stunned him completely. The doctor tugged on the small infant one limb at a time.

"Come on, you got this, cousin," Myesha bragged, fanning Jewel with her hand.

"Waaah! Waaaah!"

Everyone in the room sighed in relief.

"Whooo!" his grandmother shouted.

Bobby stood zombie-like in front of the doctor as he held his baby.

"Cut this." The doctor pointed to the cord that was connected to Jewel.

Bobby did so unblinkingly. He held his arms out. The doctor placed his baby boy into his arms. It seemed as if everyone silenced and everything paused as Bobby cradled his precious son is his arms. He was so small and fragile, forcing Bobby to be extra careful. Tears brimmed in Bobby's eyes and before he could even consider what was occurring, they descended abundantly.

***

Myesha and Dooski had come and left, and Bobby's grandmother had fallen asleep in the La-Z-Boy that was in the corner of the room. Jewel was in and out of a slumber as well. She was exhausted.

Bobby leaned against the table that he had covered with flowers, watching Jewel as she slept. Although he had yet to admit it, he held her close to his heart. She had given him something he longed for, but never had. He had never experienced love at first sight until he witnessed the birth of his son. The emptiness that lingered within didn't seem so empty anymore. He had been peering out of dull lens. It was as if his son had given him a new set of frames and suddenly, life wasn't bleak anymore. The doctor had taken Lil Bobby to the nursery, where he would be headed shortly. He wanted to be right by his side when he awakened. But first, he had something to handle.

Bobby inched closer. "Jewel," Bobby whispered, hovering over her.

Jewel stirred in her sleep, then slowly opened her eyes. "Bobby?" she whispered, quite baffled by his presence.

"Jewel, let me say this," he blurted, no longer able to contain his feelings.

Jewel sat up.

"Jewel, I love you with everything in me, and for the rest of my time here on earth, I want you and my son by my side. In regards to how I've mistreated you prior to this day, I promise to never do it again, if you just agree to love me the same."

***

Bobby left his grandmother and Jewel inside of the room to finish catching up. Jewel loved listening to her interesting remedies.

"Hey."

Bobby peered up from the phone, his brows dipped in confusion once he locked eyes with the nurse from the other day.

"Wassup?" he voiced, looking past her instead of at her.

"Um…" she hesitated. "I need you to come with me to room sixteen."

"For what?" Bobby lifted his hands in frustration. "Look, I'm about to go check on my seed. What's this about?" he continued.

"Actually, it is about your seed."

Appalled, Bobby's head jerked backwards. Confused, he trailed closely behind Kesha's friend as she led the way. He swallowed the lump in his throat before following behind her inside of the room. Immediately, he locked eyes with an exhausted Kesha. An older lady sat in the corner. She was holding a baby. The infant was no bigger than his own seed. The last thing he expected was to stop inside of a room with Kesha and her newborn. Oddly, he thought Lil Bobby would be in room sixteen.

"Hey Bobby," the older lady said.

"Hi. I mean hey, h-how are you doing?" Bobby responded, lost.

She stood. Immediately, Bobby noticed the necklace. He scowled. It was the same necklace his grandmother wore.

"I'm fine. Would you like to hold her?" She was a bit shaky, but she held onto the child for dear life. She was an older woman around his grandmother's age. She had an angelic aura about herself that Bobby immediately admired. There was no way he could tell the small woman no, so he reached out and carefully grabbed the baby, He placed her against his chest. Their heartbeats thumped rhythmically.

Goosebumps covered his arms like a bad case of poison ivy. Baffled, he held her inches away from his face. Her eyes were closed, but she was the most beautiful little girl he had ever laid eyes on. Her thick curly hair resembled his when he was merely an infant. He leaned in and sniffed the crease of her neck. The smell of babies was the one thing he adored the most. Again, tears filled his eyes as he held her close as if he was afraid she'd fall. Unintentionally, he locked eyes with Kesha. He despised her and the smirk she wore. He could be wrong and inwardly he prayed the little girl he cradled in his arms wasn't his, but something in his gut led him to believe differently.

"I have to get her back down to the nursery, but you're always welcome to go see her there."

Bobby nodded at the nurse.

Sensing the tension, the older lady stood.

"I'm going with you nurse so I can spend a few more minutes with my niece before I head back to the church."

If there were any doubts prior to who she was, they were just confirmed. Bobby's grandmother had mentioned a friend that she had at the church on several occasions. He handed the nurse the baby, then went to hug Kesha's aunt.

"It was nice meeting you. I'll be down there in a few minutes," he assured.

"Aww, okay, young man. It was nice meeting you too."

Silence filled the room as soon as they left. Disbelief lingered in the pit of his stomach. He peered at Kesha through narrow slits.

"So you didn't get that plan B?" He paced the floor, sticking his hands in the front pocket of his jeans.

Tears filled Kesha's eyes. "I couldn't afford it!" she cried.

Bobby smirked. "Bruh, you gon' lie to my face?" He inched closer.

She turned her head to the side. "Of course I'm lying." She paused. "Why am I not good enough? That girl could be your child, but she's good enough? She knows how to treat you?" She sniffed. "She's more of a woman than me? You're a liar, you're sneaky, possessive, and can't be trusted."

He shrugged.

"Wow," she mouthed.

"And again, the reason you could never level up is because you were always worried about every other bitch's position."

Kesha smacked her lips. "This is not about anyone else. We discussing you and your bullshit."

"Honestly, your role wasn't anything to exalt, but you should've, because for the longest, it was just you. I'm a man of precision. I'm not jumping from woman to woman 'cause the first time my dick gets to leaking, itching, or anything, I'll already know exactly who to go look for." He paused.

Tears brimmed in Kesha's eyes all over again as her bottom lip trembled uncontrollably.

Bobby shrugged. "Your focus should've been to excel. However, you failed your position trying to compete, when there wasn't even any competitors."

"Bobby, I'm sorry," she whined. Her face was soaked; her hair was disheveled. More exhaustion added years to her age. Yet she was still beautiful in spite of it. However, Bobby was done with her beautiful lies.

"Kesha, your sorry doesn't mean shit. No one wants to deal with a sorry motherfucka." He turned to walk away, but stopped. "I'm pretty sure that's my seed, but I want a DNA and I want one ASAP. I don't want to miss a second of either of my children's lives."

Ah'Million

CHAPTER 30
KAD

A few days had passed since the judge dismissed all of the charges against Kad. Although he was unable to witness the birth of his first and only grandson, he was elated to be a free man today. The wind grazed his face as he stood in the shade under a tree, waiting on Bobby. He was eager to see his family, but he enjoyed the scenery ahead. He shot a quick prayer to the heavens, relishing the nice breeze.

Kad scowled at the 2022 Denali approaching the curb. The window slid down.

"Damn, this you, boy?" Kad asked Bobby as he opened the passenger door.

Bobby grinned. He and Bobby cheerfully embraced, happy to see one another.

"It's good to see you out. I missed your ass," Bobby said as he drove away from the curb.

"I know. I'm ready to see my grandson and baby girl." Kad rubbed his hands together eagerly.

The mentioning of Jewel sent a wave of uneasiness over Bobby. He still hadn't told Kad about the relations between the two of them. An awkward silence filled the truck.

"Aye, turn that volume down, Bobby, and pull over to that gas station." Kad pointed to the Exxon up ahead.

Bobby nodded and veered left towards the semi-crowded gas station. Bobby nodded and did as he was told.

"So when were you gon' tell me, Bobby?" Kad asked as soon as the truck came to a stop.

Bobby sighed deeply. "I wanted to tell you face to face."

"Visitation face to face, right?"

Bobby gritted his teeth, his head swiveling at no one in particular. He daydreamed about this moment countless times so as to mentally prepare himself. Hearing the sarcasm in Kad's voice, he knew right then things wouldn't be as simple as he imagined.

"Right. Look, Kad, that was foul." He held his hands up in surrender. "But I love Jewel with all of my heart and soul." He placed his right hand on top of his chest.

"You know, Jewel told me months ago and I'm glad she did, 'cause I had time to ponder on it all." Kad caressed the hairs on his chin.

Bobby's brow raised. Jewel hadn't mentioned it to him that she told Kad anything

You took a bullet for my baby girl." He jabbed his chest. "You did something I should've been out there doing, but I was in a jail cell behind a bitch. I commend you. This the second time you did something for me that I should've did myself, causing you detriment in the process!"

Bobby's face was solid, yet inwardly, he was relieved.

"I've known you for a long time, Bobby. You're a man of few words, a lot of actions, and scarce emotions. For you to confirm how you feel with your mouth in a way you never spoke about a female other than your mother, I know it's real."

Bobby lowered his head.

Simultaneously, they grinned and slapped hands, pulling each other in for a hug.

"'Preciate ya, man. I've been stressing like a motherfucka." He chuckled

Ring! Ring! ,Ring!

"This Jewel right here," Bobby continued. "Hello?"

"Baby, get here now, something is wrong with Lil Bobby."

CHAPTER 31
JEWEL

"Just calm ya nerves, chile," Ms. Taylor advised, sitting beside Jewel on the sofa. She had been staying at Bobby's place since the hospital released Jewel and Lil Bobby.

They peered in the direction of the door, hearing the locks click. Bobby and Kad rushed inside.

"Daddy!" Jewel screamed like a young child. The sadness in her eyes vanished momentarily as she flew into her father's arms.

"Hey baby girl, what's the matter?" His eyes moved swiftly.

"What's wrong with him?" Bobby asked.

"I think he has a sinus infection or something. I peeped it yesterday, but I thought I was overreacting so I didn't say anything." The winkles that marked her forehead were a clear indication of her insurmountable stress.

Bobby covered Jewel's hand with his. "Come on, let's go see about him. Come on, Granny," Bobby continued.

***

"Ms. McVale, what seems to be the problem?" the pediatrician asked.

"His breathing patterns are slightly off. I think he has a sinus infection or something," Jewel voiced, allowing the doctor to check and monitor Lil Bobby's breathing.

Nearly twenty minutes later, she turned to Jewel and said, "I don't think it's anything too concerning, but I'll do a check-up in two weeks, or stop by if it seems to worsen."

They left the hospital and returned home. Bobby and Kad immediately began to discuss business as Jewel retired to the bedroom.

"What are you doing?" she asked Myesha.

"Girl, I'm at work! Where's my baby?"

Jewel sighed. "He's right here. He's fine."

Myesha had done a complete one-eighty since being released from jail. She was a waitress at Buffalo Wild Wings at night and braided hair during the day. She even made plans to attend night classes to attain her diploma.

"Okay, give him a kiss for me."

"Will do. How is Aunty Bey?"

"She's coming around. I've been ripping and running, helping her get everything together for the funeral."

"How's Bianca?"

"Um, she is just trying to be strong. I know she fucked up. I see it in her eyes. She probably was mad at Brandi, but there was a lot of love there."

"Well, if you need anything, I can help. My dad is home now, so I got super support." Myesha chuckled.

"I love you, girl, so much, and I'll call you as soon as I make it home. Give my love to everyone."

Bobby marched inside, his face distorted in contempt. He cleared his throat.

Jewel's smile slowly faded until it was completely gone. "What is it, bae?"

"Jewel, we need to talk."

Bobby closed the door behind him as he stepped completely inside. He swallowed the lump in his throat, carefully considering the best way to tell Jewel while causing the least harm. However, there was no way to voice the truth without offending his shorty.

"Sit down, bae," he suggested, eyeing her intently.

Jewel shook her head as tears brimmed in her eyes. "No, Bobby, I want to stand, Just tell me."

Bobby pinched his bottom lip and sighed deeply. He paced the floor aggressively, palming his waves. "Kesha just had a little girl." He lowered his head. "She told me she was mine." He paused.

Jewel eased down onto the bed. Her breathing ceased. Bobby wanted to rush to her aid, but he had already started he couldn't stop now.

"I told her to holla at me when she get the DNA." He paused, shifting right to left. "Well, the results came in earlier." He paused. "She mine, Jewel."

CHAPTER 32
BOBBY

Bobby held Lil Bobby in one arm and Bria in the other. Jewel didn't voice it, but the revelation of Bria troubled her deeply, and Bobby knew it. Even when he would ask her things to pick her brain, she would downplay it, but her actions revealed otherwise. She wasn't as talkative or opinionated. That beautiful smile he had fallen in love with was scarce as food in Africa. She had become impassive.

He sat on the sofa and reclined against the pillows, admiring both of his children as they peacefully slept. Although he tried concealing it, it bothered him knowing that he was the sole purpose for Jewel's heartache.

"I'm ready," Jewel called out, standing beside the food. Today was the day they would see the pediatrician again for Lil Bobby's checkup.

***

Bobby and Jewel sat inside of the small but roomy doctor's office. Bobby placed a hand on Jewel's lap to cease her leg from vibrating.

"Chill, bae, everything is going to be okay," he assured.

Jewel peered in his direction and rolled her eyes. She didn't have on a lick of makeup. Her face was bare. Her eyes were swollen.

Doctor Tolett's brows dipped in confusion. "His head seems to be growing a little too quickly. We're going to have to run some tests."

An hour or so later, Bobby and Jewel returned home with Lil Bobby. Jewel sobbed silently the entire drive from the hospital. Bobby assumed that Jewel was being a typical female, allowing her emotions to run wild simply because in spite of the doctor's speculations, he knew without a shadow of a doubt that his son would be just fine.

He tossed his keys on the dining room table. Jewel and Lil Bobby retreated to the back. Bobby dragged towards the extra bedroom his grandmother was sleeping in. He could hear the snoring outside of the door. However, as soon as he opened the door her snoring ceased and her eyes fluttered open.

"Wha-what happened?" she inquired, rubbing the sleep out of her eyes. She hadn't returned home since Lil Bobby was born. She scooted up against the headboard.

Bobby took a seat on the edge of her bed. "They ran a few tests. Doc said his head is rather big for his age. The results will be in a week or two from now."

Ms. Taylor smacked her lips and waved Bobby off. "That boy is fine. He get that big ole head from you," she joked. Her laughter faded into a nasty cough.

Bobby rushed to her aid, handing her the bottled water on the nightstand.

"Thank you, baby," she whispered breathlessly after taking a swig. "Tomorrow, I want you to take me to the church. Me and all my sisters going to lift Lil Bobby up in prayer."

Bobby nodded. "Yes ma'am."

He slowly lifted off the edge of the bed and walked to the side where his grandmother lay. He planted a soft kiss on her forehead. "I love you, Granny. Me and Lil Bobby about to go see Kad."

"Okay, baby, I'll see you when you get back."

Bobby left and went inside of the room he and Jewel shared. Lil Bobby lay curled beneath her chin, bottoms up. Jewel arm draped over his small frame. He picked Lil Bobby up, sliding him directly underneath her arm.

Jewel immediately jumped up, but as soon as she locked eyes with Bobby, her shoulders slumped and her nerves calmed.

"We'll be back," he mumbled, placing him gently on the shoulder.

"Where are y'all going?"

"To see his granddaddy. Lay down and get some sleep."

Jewel didn't protest. She nodded and lay back down. "Be careful," she whispered, never taking her eyes off them.

Bobby grabbed the baby tote they had taken to the doctor visit. He threw it across his shoulder and headed out. He tossed the bag in the back with the stroller. He opened the door to the driver's seat and slowly climbed in with his son lying against his chest.

The engine came alive and the Durk lyrics filled the 2022 Denali. He gently lifted Lil Bobby off his chest and held him a few inches from his face. Lil Bobby's small hands were curled into a fist as he rubbed them over his small and slightly swollen eyes. Bobby examined his every move and his supposedly enlarged head.

"Yo' shit look pretty normal to me," Bobby voiced.

A half-smile etched Lil Bobby's face. The small gesture warmed Bobby's heart.

He held him closer, squeezing him a bit. "Let's go see Papa," Bobby said.

He cradled Bobby in his left arm and steered the wheel with his right, bobbing his head to the Lil Durk lyrics that filled his Denali.

"These tears shed whenever he dead
Its different seein' 'em die (boc)
Get close up on 'em you know dat shyt be graphic
You gotta pop out with the ratchet
You know this shit gets tragic.
And you can't fumble with the stick…"

***

A week later, Bobby and Jewel returned to the hospital, seated in the same office as they awaited the results in regards to Lil Bobby's health

"Mr. and Ms. McVale, I'm sorry to be the bearer of bad news." He paused. "But your son has been diagnosed with high-grade glioma."'

Bobby's and Jewel's heads turned swiftly as they locked eyes. Their expressions resembled matching patterns as they shared the same sadden and confused look.

"What's that, Doc?"

Doctor Tollet lowered his head, placing his hands inside the pockets of his lab coat. "It's a rare and aggressive form of brain cancer." He paused.

Bobby's and Jewel's brows dipped in confusion. Bobby instantly stopped breathing. The word cancer rang loudly and repeatedly in his head.

"High-grade gliomas are tumors found in the brain and spinal cord. These tumors can grow and spread quickly. Eight to twelve percent of all childhood brain tumors and their cause remain unknown."

Tears quickly filled and fell from their eyes.

"Aaargghhh!" Bobby screamed. He curled his fist into a ball, squeezing his eyes shit. "I'm dreaming, I'm dreaming," he mumbled. "Tell me the shit a dream." His voice ascended. Tell me it's not real!" he yelled, opening his eyes. "No, no, no, no, no, this my seed, Doc," he whined into the palm of his hands. "So D-Doctor, there is nothing at all we can do?"

Doctor Tollet shook his head slowly and sighed deeply, lowering his head. You could tell the doctor enjoyed everything about his job but this.

"I'm afraid not. My advice is to create moments of joy every day for him." He paused. "It could be weeks, or it could be months. I'm so sorry, guys." He was sorry, and what perturbed him the most was the fact he couldn't cure the helpless child from the rare disease. "It's very difficult to treat the disease. I could try chemotherapy. However, I promise to do all that I can to keep him breathing and alive for as long as possible. The chemo can extend his life expectancy but he'll suffer in the process. Chemo is difficult for adults."

Kad took the news hard. However, it didn't compare to how hard Ms. Taylor took it. You would've thought she was Mary and Lil Bobby was baby Jesus.

A family gathering was held at Bobby's. Kesha's aunt came as well. The atmosphere was gloomy, like the morning of a funeral.

"I know no one is feeling this and you'd rather grieve, but we have to take it to the altar. Let His will be done," she quoted holding her hand out.

Everyone around the table held hands allowing the small but powerful woman pray over Lil Bobby.

Both Jewel and Bobby had been quite despondent, barely enough help for each other. Kad and Myesha visited quite often to assist them with Lil Bobby. However, they simply wanted to hold him tightly until they were no longer able to. The both of them figured that there was no way he could die in their arms, so they figured they'd hold him forever. Hope was the only thing left, and they clung to it like their last breath.

It was days since the visit with Doctor Tollet. The three of them lay in bed. Lil Bobby and Jewel were fast asleep. Bobby lay awake, savoring the most beautiful moment his eyes will ever see, unsure and afraid that soon the image wouldn't be so vivid. He watched their chests rise and fall. Bobby scowled as Lil Bobby squirmed. He opened his small mouth. He appeared to be gasping for air. Bobby placed a hand on his chest. Immediately, he noticed his abnormal breathing pattern. There was a pause in his breathing, perhaps five to ten seconds then a huge gasp. Bobby froze, frightened. Things were definitely taking a turn for the worse.

His chest tightened and a fearful yet familiar sensation engulfed him. Thoughts of the day he received the news about the death of his father surfaced. He gripped the sheet underneath him in an attempt to overcome the nasty storm brewing.

Gently, he shook Jewel. Jewel jerked forward. Her eyes widened in fear.

"Bae, let's go out on the porch and watch the sunrise." His words were laced with defeat and initially, Jewel was quite lost, but the pain in his eyes ceased her question and concerns and instantly tears fell from both their eyes two at a time. She knew eventually it would happen, but she hated the fact that it was her family having to endure such tragedy.

Without uttering a word, they both silently dressed. It was a few minutes past four. She lifted up. Bobby closed his eyes and pressed his face in his hands. All the money, power, and respect he accumulated over his life span was nothing but a bunch of smoke because none of it could save his son. Bobby never took his eyes off Lil

Bobby as he pulled the shirt down over his head, and neither did Jewel. Sniffles filled the room as Jewel and Bobby dressed themselves in the dark. Light from the clock and phone screens were the only things that illuminated the room. Bobby gently picked up Lil Bobby and cradled him into his arms, savoring his scent and innocence in the process.

Tears blurred his vision. Jewel rested her nose in the crease of his neck.

"Here." Bobby handed Lil Bobby to Jewel. "Meet me on the porch. I'm going to wake up Granny." Bobby used his T-shirt to dry his drenched face, then eased inside of his grandmother's room. She was knelt down beside the bed praying.

She felt it.

Moments later, she struggled to her feet, using the bed for leverage. Tears soiled her aging face as she gave Bobby a tight-lipped smile. With her hands clasped in front of her, she gritted her teeth to gain control of her tears,

"I'm so sorry, son." She pointed. "One thing you must understand is the man upstairs makes no mistakes." Tears continue to fall as the salty liquid glided between her lips.

"Yes ma'am." Bobby nodded. He felt like a peon. However, no amount of fight in the world could save Lil Bobby. It was like knowing the day and time of the world ending. It simply was impossible.

"Come on." Bobby grabbed his grandmother's plump hand and led the way.

The four of them gathered on the porch. Jewel and Bobby sat side by side on the steps and Ms. Taylor sat in the rocking chair. Lil Bobby lay in both Jewel's and Bobby's arms, a half-smile plastered on his face. He didn't seem to have a care in the world. Every so often Jewel and Bobby would peck his forehead. The breeze grazed his cheek. He lifted his head and looked to the west. The sky was a combination of pink, orange, and red. He had seen the sunrise countless times, but there was something different about today. He tightened his jaw. His chest swelled. Something told him everything would be different after today. He inhaled deeply and peered down at his creation. He wanted to mentally capture the image forever.

The fresh angelic scent rose, lingering around his nostrils he pulled Lil Bobby closer. He wanted to forever remember his smell as well.

The sun was beginning to rise and Lil Bobby's breathing seemed to improve. Bobby began to feel optimistic. The three of them engaged in minimal conversation. Lil Bobby's lips were curled into a smile.

"That chile look so peaceful," Ms. Taylor commented. "Can I see him?"

Bobby looked at Jewel for approval. She softly nodded and released the half of Lil Bobby that she cradled. Bobby climbed the two steps and placed him into his grandmother's arms. She sighed deeply and moaned softly. She wrapped her plump arms around Lil Bobby's tiny frame as her tears streamed down her face and on top of his head.

"God has so much in store for you baby He saving you from the evil of this world and soon we'll be reunited," she rambled softly. "Soon and very soon, we are going to see the king." She repeatedly sang the church hymn.

Jewel broke down. Bobby wrapped his arm around her neck pulling her head into his neck softly she cried on his shoulder.

Minutes passed and Bobby noticed his grandmother had stopped humming, Slowly he turned around. Her hand was pressed against the back of his head. Her face was soaked, her cheek pressed against his. His breathing stopped, his voice inaudible. He turned back around and lightly tapped Jewel. The tap felt as painful and dreadful as stabs. Immediately, she knew what they meant.

The three of them mourned Lil Bobby silently, then his grandmother prayed for him.

The night after Lil Bobby passed, Jewel and Bobby cuddled in bed, neither of them asleep. Jewel turned to face Bobby.

"Bobby?" she asked.

"Hmmm?"

"I know I wasn't as receptive at first, but after the funeral I would like to help you raise La'Bria."

Bobby was baffled. "Really?"

"Yeah, 'cause I can't guarantee you that I'm going to try to give you another child right now because I'm scared." She paused, a single tear escaping her eyes. "I have to heal first, and honestly I don't know how long that's going to take."

Bobby nodded in agreement, smiling on the inside. That was the best news he heard since the visit.

"Jewel, will you marry me?"

Slowly, Jewel pulled away from him. Her brows rose in amazement. "Are you serious?"

Any remaining doubts ceased the moment she exalted selflessness, placing her feelings aside to accommodate his. Her sacrifices had finally granted her the peace and prosperity she longed for.

"As serious as I'll ever be. I love you, Jewel." He leaned in and pressed his succulent lips against hers.

She invited him inside her warmth, holding nothing back.

"Yes, I'd love to be your wife, Bobby."

CHAPTER 33
MYESHA

Myesha lay under her sheets in a deep slumber when a text came through, awakening her instantly. She realized she had fallen asleep as she sat up in her bed and peered around her bedroom for Dooski.

He's still not here.

She picked up her phone and checked her text. Dooski had left home two hours ago.

Dooski: Bae, I'm pulling in the apartment unlock the door.

Bey had been at her place since the morning she found out Brandi had been brutally murdered. Seeing her mother asleep on the sofa, it dawned on her that she hadn't mourned her sister. She had tried. She spent many hours recalling good times, hoping she'd shed a tear or two. So much for wishful thinking.

She rushed to the window and peered out of the blinds. She placed a hand over her heart, hoping it'd cease the clamoring inside of her chest. Peering out into the darkness, there was no sign of Dooski.

Where is he?

The door flew open. Myesha gasped sharply. It was Dooski. The light seeping through the tattered blinds beamed inches above his head. Sweat beads covered his forehead.

"You scared me," she whispered.

Dooski rushed inside, locking the door behind him, cloaked in fear and paranoia. It frightened Myesha instantly.

"What's wrong?" she whispered, not wanting to wake her mother. The last thing she need was an interrogation.

Dooski lifted his hands, placing them on top of his head. He deeply sighed.

"I killed him, bae," he confessed, locking eyes with the one whom he trusted with everything.

Myesha nodded slowly, tucking both lips inside her mouth so that Dooski wouldn't see them quiver. She knew this day would come, yet she also thought she was prepared. She tightened her jaws to refrain from panicking. However, inwardly, she was as shook as a sinner reading Revelations.

"Shit went far from smooth, bae," he added, never breaking his stare. "That bullshit-ass Beretta jammed and I was this close…" He paused, holding up his thumb and index finger, emphasizing the severity of the inside, "…to getting my shit pushed back," he finished loudly.

Myesha pressed her fingers to her lips. She peered back at her mother. Bey squirmed, but she never opened her eyes. Gently, Myesha guided Dooski inside of their bedroom. He flopped onto the bed.

"It's okay." Myesha stood in between his legs as she planted kisses on his sweaty forehead. "You're alive and you handled your business."

"Yeah. Now my nigga can rest easy."

CHAPTER 34
BEY

Bey tiptoed back to the couch with a mischievous smirk permanently etched on her saggy face. She stopped the recording as she sat on the sofa and saved it to her phone. She tossed the cover over her head to muffle out the sound as she dialed the numbers 9-1-1.

"How may I help you?"

"I'd like to report a murder."

"I'm listening."

"There was a shooting maybe thirty minutes to an hour ago. The shooter drives a black Charger and he's at 2622 Beltline Drive, apartment number 228, Dallas, TX 75206. And I also have a recording of him verbally admitting his crime."

"We'll send someone right over. Be careful and stay put."

Bey eased the cover down slowly to see if anyone had been listening. Seeing that the coast was clear, she smiled wickedly.

Eye for an eye and a man for a man. You put my guy in a box, and I'm putting yours in a can.

Bey lay curled up on the couch. She forced her eyes shut as they twitched rapidly. Anxiously, her feet shook involuntarily.

The door to Myesha's bedroom opened and Bey instantly felt a knot in the pit of her stomach. She couldn't wait for Myesha to suffer the way she had. There was nothing pleasant about losing a loved one, and now it was her turn to experience the heartache.

"Momma!"

Bey gasped sharply. She was expecting her daughter, but the deep baritone was the total opposite of what she had expected.

"Calm down, Momma," Dooski voiced in a low tone as he placed his index finger up to his lips. "Shhh! Shhh! It's just me," he continued as he squatted down beside the couch, eye level with her.

Bey placed a hand over her chest as she peered into Dooski's big brown eyes. They were different. Oddly different. Multiple emotions crammed them, yet fear stood out amongst them all. Bey had never seen Dooski so troubled.

"Boy, you scared me." She sat up, swallowing the lump in her throat.

"Ma…" Dooski paused. Sweat beads decorated his forehead and the space underneath his nose. Dooski hesitated, his head swiveling in the direction opposite of Bey.

"What, boy?"

He placed his phone on the coffee table next to him. Dooski clenched his teeth and he locked eyes with Bey. "Momma, I'm going to leave for a little while." His bottom lip quivered as tears brimmed his eyes. "Please, please." He brought his hands together like people do when they pray. "Take care of Myesha for me."

She had braced herself for what he might say, but that was the last thing she expected. Jealousy coupled with pity. Bey's eyes shifted in every direction but Dooski's. She was jealous as she perceived the love that the man in front of her had for her baby girl. Every strand of hair on his head, every limb in his body, was devoted to her, and it bothered her that she was twice her daughter's age and hadn't experienced anything like it. However, she felt horrible for what was yet to come.

"Baby, you look like you in trouble." Bey jumped to her feet. She knew the police would be there at any second.

"Yes ma'am, I am." He lowered his head.

"Well, go on." Bey waved. "Go on and get. I got Myesha. You like the son I never had. I got you too. But if you in some trouble now, you need to go." A few minutes ago, she thought she wanted vengeance, but the tears of the impassive man before her softened her heart, making her regret her impulsive decision.

Dooski leaned in and hugged Bey tightly. Her guilt only worsened. He jogged towards the door, scooped the duffle bag up beside it, and hurried out the front door.

Bey ran and peaked out the window. Her hands trembled as her eyes roamed the darkness, hoping the police hadn't showed up. She stood in the window and watched until Dooski swerved out of the lot. Bey rushed inside of Myesha's room. Sniffles filled the room as she lay on her stomach. Her body heaved. Bey climbed on top of the bed and lay next to her baby girl.

"Police! Open up!"

Ah'Million

CHAPTER 35
KAD

Days had passed since the death of his first grandson. It was time that he get back to business but first him and Ms. Mayes had business of their own to tend to. Since being released, he learned a few things about "Ms. Mayes", and in spite of the sorrow he endured lately, he looked forward to seeing her.

Kad anxiously tapped the steering wheel as he kept checking his mirrors. He looked down at his watch to check the time and noticed that it was a few minutes past noon. Mercedes was late for their lunch date. Other than her beauty, it was still something that he was drawn to. He just hadn't figured it out yet. He wanted to learn more about her.

Just as he was about to start up his car and pull off, he saw a truck that matched the description whip into the lot. He grinned, inwardly admitting the joy in seeing her.

Mercedes pulled up next to him, exposing her beautiful smile. "Hey." she said.

"Hey sexy," Kad replied.

"Sorry I'm late. I had to take my son over my mother's house."

"He good?"

"Yeah, he fine."

"Well, come on," he said, extending his hand.

Mercedes placed her hand inside of his and Kad led her inside of the restaurant. He peered around to check out the busy establishment. It was his first time at the soul food restaurant. He assumed she had been there countless times.

A waitress walked up hovering over them. Mercedes ordered without picking up her menu, confirming his assumption. "You ready?" the waitress asked Kad.

"I'll have the same thing she's having," he answered, never taking his eyes off Mercedes.

He was slightly nervous. Mercedes was by far the most beautiful woman he had ever seen. He wanted her in the worst way, yet he promised himself that he'd take it slow. Although Mercedes didn't seem like the type to play grimy games just to come up off a brother's paper, his prior situation had him given trust issues.

Ms. Independent.

Her skin was smooth and her lips were full. He would catch himself staring. *Fuck.* He couldn't help it.

Mercedes peered up and caught Kad watching her. "What's up, Kad?"

"What's up, Mercedes?"

She chuckled at the sound of her name. "Hmph, first name basis?" She shrugged. "That's fine with me," she continued, not giving him a chance to respond.

Kad picked at the dumplings. The food smelled delicious, but he hadn't regained his appetite since the death of his grandson.

"What's on your mind?" she asked. Her eyes filled with concern.

Kad shrugged. "It's nothing. Nothing I can't handle."

His strength was attractive. Having prior dealings with so many weak dudes, she caught herself thinking of what it would be like if Kad was her man. So many times she had to dominate instead of submit or simply have all of the answers instead of the questions. She was a good woman and she deserved her equal her king. Kad was a king. In spite of his charges and the circumstances she met him under, it took nothing from his image. He was something special. His Savage Dior cologne lingered.

Kad reached over and grabbed her hand, it was as if their souls connected instantly. Kad gazed into her eyes, never breaking the stare. Everything about her was perfect to him.

"I want you bad as I want my next breath, but just bear with me," he voiced in admiration. Her thick frame and wide hips made Kad's mind think about what they were going to do after they left. Her full lips and made-up face made her resemble a ghetto Barbie.

"Can I ask you a question?" he asked.

"Anything," she answered.

Ring! Ring! Ring!

Kad slowly used his free hand to reach into his pocket and retrieve his phone. He squinted at the number on the screen. "Hello?"

"You have a collect call from Beatrice."

Kad quickly accepted the call cutting the phone operator short. "Hello, hello?"

"Bey, what is going on?" Kad asked, barely able to hear himself because of the drums in his chest

"Look, I don't have a clue what's going on, but I'm in Dallas County Jail. The police picked up me and Myesha from her house." She spoke as fast as she could on the free sixty second call.

"They just picked y'all up?" Kad inquired, scowling, somewhat confused about what was occurring. "Do y'all have a bond?"

"We haven't been to court yet, but supposedly it's just for questioning."

"Alright, hold tight, I'm——"

"Your call has ended. Goodbye," the operator chimed in, cutting Kad off.

If it's not one thing, it's another. He sighed deeply.

Mercedes read Kad's expression. He hated to leave so suddenly and she hated to watch him leave.

"Don't trip. Go and handle your business. There is always tomorrow. Besides, I have to be at that motherfucka bright and early," she said, slowly standing to her feet.

This was the only peace of mind Kad had gotten this week. Chilling with Mercedes had taken his mind off all of the apprehension that crammed it. "You sure?" Kad stood as well.

"I'm positive. I'm a big girl," she replied walking into his personal space, then wrapping her arms around his neck. The smell of her subtle but lingering Jo Malone fragrance instantly attacked his nostrils, making the vein in his dick come alive.

Damn, Bey always fucking my shit up.

"You better be ready tomorrow," he whispered as he hugged her tightly.

She closed her eyes and savored his cologne. They stared at each other smiling for a few seconds before peeling apart.

"You deserve the world, Mercedes," Kad said with sincerity.

His charm melted her, and it was so effortless with Kad. "Handle your business and I'll see tomorrow." She stood on her tiptoes to give him a peck on the lips.

Kad gently smacked her ass and squeezed it just before sliding his phone into his pocket and heading towards the exit.

CHAPTER 36
DOOSKI

"Ain't have nobody to give me no hope,
I hope my momma ain't doing no coke
I used to wish that my daddy was living
I had a dream that I seen him as a ghost..."

Dooski drove along the highway with blood-drenched clothing and all of his windows rolled down as Meek blasted through the speakers. It was as if he was in a daze. His whole life had changed in the blink of an eye.

He pulled out his phone to call Bobby. Since losing Blotchy, there wasn't a soul he could trust besides Myesha. However, there was an aura about Bobby that put him at ease. Like the old saying goes, "real recognizes real", and it definitely didn't take long for Dooski to peep it. He swiped his thumb across the screen to unlock the phone as he pulled into the lot of the IHOP.

What the fuck?

The screen unlocked without him giving his password. Instantly, he realized he had mistakenly picked up Bey's phone instead of his own. It was senseless to try and figure out Bobby's number. Surely, he wouldn't remember it. He could call Myesha and get the number from her, but opted against it. He placed the phone inside of the cup holder and sped off the lot. He had no plans of pulling up on Bobby, but he was left no choice.

Dooski sat in Bobby's driveway with his two F&Ns on his lap. Paranoid was an understatement. His eyes frantically rocked from left to right while watching any and everything that moved on the oddly quiet street. He knew Bobby's place was safe for now. He just needed a few minutes to clean his head, or at least try to. He stepped out of his whip and like a thief in the night, he eased up the clear path and then up the stairs. His knock was light, so light that if they weren't paying attention, it could possibly go unheard. He didn't want to alarm them though.

"Boy, you almost got shot," Bobby said once he opened the door and spotted Dooski. You could tell by the way his chest heaved that he wasn't expecting his visit.

Dooski said nothing.

"What's going on? Get in here."

Dooski stepped inside and immediately Bobby noticed the bloodstained shirt and lost look in his eyes.

"I killed 'em B. I killed him," Dooski admitted through vacant eyes.

"Killed who?"

"The nigga that clapped at you and Blotchy. I had to. I wasn't sloppy with it, but something in my gut is telling me that I need to move around for a couple days," Dooski said as he looked into Bobby eyes.

Bobby bit down on his lip. As badly as he wanted to stay out of it and leave Dooski to fend for himself, he simply couldn't.

"Always go with your gut. It's the only thing that will never lead you astray. Give me a second."

Dooski peered out of the blinds once Bobby was out of his sight.

"Here." He returned and handed Dooski the keys to his Lexus. It was a later model than his Escalade, but he couldn't turn the keys to his Lac over.

Dooski peered at him, dumbfounded.

"Take mine and leave yours here. It's too hot right now."

"Bet. Look, I need you to give this to Bey somehow. I grabbed it by accident," Dooski said, placing the phone in his hand.

"Cool, I got you." Dooski turned to leave, but not without his hesitation going unnoticed.

Bobby watched Dooski from the middle of the living room. Effortlessly, he conveyed the irreparable feeling he must've felt.

"Aye fam!" Bobby called out.

Slowly, Dooski turned to face him. Doubt weighed heavy on his mind, but he'd never admit it.

"It's up there with us. You family now. Whichever way this shit go, you gon' be good. Head up, chest out."

"No doubt," Dooski voiced. A half-smile etched his face as he walked out of Bobby's feeling reassured.

Ah'Million

CHAPTER 37
BOBBY

Jewel and Bobby lay cuddled up on top of covers when the two of them should have been tending to other important matters.

"Bae, you know what I find so baffling?" Jewel asked. Her intent was to never bring it up, but like bad gas, she just had to let it out. Holding it in was simply frustrating.

"What, bae?"

She turned around to face him so that she could see the look in his eyes after revealing the harsh reality. "Blotchy was so upset when he found out that Dooski had gotten signed that he——" she cleared her throat. "He, he mentioned killing him. He figured without Dooski, he had a chance of possibly getting signed again."

Bobby's brows crimped in confusion. "Woooowww," he said, then let out a chuckle. He shook his head. "Love don't love nobody," he voiced aloud. He felt pity for Dooski. He was thorough, a man of integrity. He did something he needed to do, even though he didn't have to. In this world, no one has to do anything, but if someone popped yo' homie, family, or loved one and you knew about it and he was still breathing, you ain't a hunnid, period.

"He gon' be alright. He can show his face again when shit dies down."

"Police! Open up!"

Both Jewel and Bobby jerked forward, fear engulfing them, Jewel mainly. He grabbed her by the face, slowing the pace of her rapidly beating heart.

"Shhh! You good. I got this."

She nodded quickly.

Bobby rushed to the door to answer it before they kicked it down.

"What's up?" Bobby slightly opened the door wide enough to stick his head out.

The white male officer stood in front of the door with his hands on his hip, and his buddy wasn't too far behind him.

"Sir, we traced a call that was placed almost an hour ago and that car there…" He pointed to Dooski's Charger in the driveway.

"…matches the description that we were given."

Bobby swallowed the lump in his throat. He didn't know if they were lying or telling the truth. He was beginning to question Dooski. Then the thought vanished as quickly as it appeared. There was no way Dooski led them to his spot and if so, they would've gotten him while he was here.

"Sorry, officers, I don't know what you're talking about, but if you come back with a search warrant, I will gladly to comply."

They nodded slowly.

"You won't have no choice then, boy," the cop said as he descended the steps.

Bobby slammed the door shut. "Suck my dick." He turned around, almost bumping into a frightened Jewel.

"What the hell, Bobby?" Tears fell two at a time and her bottom lip quivered uncontrollably. "I can't lose you, Bobby!" She leaned into his chest and sobbed.

He wrapped his toned arms around her. "Bae, I'm not going nowhere," he assured, gently patting her on the back. He pulled back and gripped her shoulders. Her face was soaked. "Jewel, I need you to be strong for me. It's some shit going on and I need to get to the bottom of it."

He moved past her and towards the counter where he had set Bey's phone. He knew damn well neither he nor Jewel placed it, so it had to have come from Bey's phone. He prayed that she wouldn't have a password, and she didn't. He scrolled to her outgoing calls and sure enough, there it was. He shook his head. Bey was never going to change. He couldn't understand why she did the shit she did. He wished he could hear the conversation that transpired between Bey and the operator.

There was a knock at the door. Bobby turned around swiftly. His eyes widened in bewilderment. He locked eyes with Jewel, giving her the okay to open it. He aimed his Glock inches above her head, ready in case some shit popped off.

"Hey baby, you okay?" Kad asked, placing his hands on her cheeks.

Bobby lowered his gun at the sound of Kad's voice.

"I'm okay, Daddy."

"Come on, y'all ride with me. They got Bey and Myesha," he informed. You could tell he was spooked.

Bobby's shoulders slumped as he lowered his head. "Jewel, let me——"

"No, I'm not a child, Bobby, and besides, I already know what's going on! I'm scared as hell right now. I don't want to be alone." Jewel crossed her arms over her chest. She resembled a bad-ass kid throwing a temper tantrum.

"You right. Come here." He held her tightly as he began to inform Kad about what exactly what was going on.

"So, Bey snitched?" Kad asked in shock. He simply couldn't believe what he was hearing.

Bobby didn't respond. He just simply lifted the phone, showing her outgoing call list.

Kad shook his head in disbelief. "The hell wrong with Bey? I'm about to take my ass home. I'll see you tomorrow, boy." He slapped hands with Bobby. Bey was his sister, but these days, the word family held no weight. "Baby, I'll take you tomorrow to get Myesha out," he said before planting a kiss on her forehead.

Jewel nodded calmly, wrapping her arms around her father.

Ah'Million

CHAPTER 38
A FEW WEEKS LATER

The smell of warm vanilla burned throughout the home, mixed with the scent of marijuana. Myesha took a pull as she bobbed her head to the Kehlani lyrics. Her hair was wrapped in a multicolored head wrap, and only the soft baby hair that rested on her edges were visible.

Dooski stared at her from across the table. The two of them had just finished their meal. Nigeria wasn't exactly what Myesha expected, but she couldn't care less. She would've gone to hell if someone would've told her Dooski was going to be there.

She and Bey were released the day after they were taken into custody. Neither one of them was charged. However, Bey volunteered enough information to bury Dooski, in fear that they would attempt to jail her for withholding such information. Once Myesha learned Dooski's location, they were face to face in a matter of days. He had been better to her than her own family, and that's why she made the conscious decision of choosing him. Of course, Jewel and Bianca would be missed, but they all were living their own lives. She had found a man that loved her more than he loved himself. Only a fool would disregard such rare entity.

Dooski and Myesha walked outside onto the porch. Myesha rubbed her protruding belly as she eyed the young girls jump-roping barefoot. Unaware of their situations and the formalities that didn't exist because of their adversity, they laughed and played without a care in the world.

Some of the houses had openings where windows should have been. Roofs were damaged and each house looked to be on its last leg.

Dooski gazed into her eyes as he rubbed her stomach. His tattooed body was on full display. His artwork was part of his new disguise. His belly hung slightly over his belt buckle. It wasn't big as it once was. His new Keto was really working for him.

"I love you, Queen." He smiled, revealing his beautiful teeth, which were highlighted by his neatly-trimmed full beard - another addition to his appearance to disguise the fugitive he had become.

"I love you too. my king."

Ring! Ring! Ring!

Myesha pulled out and then answered her phone.

"Hey girl."

"Heyyy, your ass better be on the plane."

"We're all at the airport."

Different voices sent their greetings through the small speaker.

They were a few days shy of their big day. Dooski and Myesha would wed, and so would Bobby and Jewel, with Kad and Mercedes in attendance. It wasn't anything like the wedding they may have dreamed of, but to them, their union was a dream coming true - a vow that united and did not break them in spite of typical and even uncommon and uncontrollable mishaps.

The End

Lock Down Publications and Ca$h Presents assisted publishing packages.

BASIC PACKAGE $499
Editing
Cover Design
Formatting

UPGRADED PACKAGE $800
Typing
Editing
Cover Design
Formatting

ADVANCE PACKAGE $1,200
Typing
Editing
Cover Design
Formatting
Copyright registration
Proofreading
Upload book to Amazon

LDP SUPREME PACKAGE $1,500
Typing
Editing
Cover Design
Formatting
Copyright registration
Proofreading
Set up Amazon account
Upload book to Amazon

Ah'Million

Advertise on LDP Amazon and Facebook page

***Other services available upon request. Additional charges may apply
Lock Down Publications
P.O. Box 944
Stockbridge, GA 30281-9998
Phone # 470 303-9761

Submission Guideline

Submit the first three chapters of your completed manuscript to ldpsubmissions@gmail.com, subject line: Your book's title. The manuscript must be in a .doc file and sent as an attachment. Document should be in Times New Roman, double spaced and in size 12 font. Also, provide your synopsis and full contact information. If sending multiple submissions, they must each be in a separate email.

Have a story but no way to send it electronically? You can still submit to LDP/Ca$h Presents. Send in the first three chapters, written or typed, of your completed manuscript to:

LDP: Submissions Dept
Po Box 944
Stockbridge, Ga 30281

DO NOT send original manuscript. Must be a duplicate.

Provide your synopsis and a cover letter containing your full contact information.

Thanks for considering LDP and Ca$h Presents.

<u>NEW RELEASES</u>

BLOOD AND GAMES by KING DREAM

SOSA GANG 3 by ROMELL TUKES

IT'S JUST ME AND YOU 2 by AH'MILLION

Coming Soon from Lock Down Publications/Ca$h Presents

BLOOD OF A BOSS **VI**

SHADOWS OF THE GAME II

TRAP BASTARD II

By **Askari**

LOYAL TO THE GAME **IV**

By **T.J. & Jelissa**

TRUE SAVAGE **VIII**

MIDNIGHT CARTEL IV

DOPE BOY MAGIC IV

CITY OF KINGZ III

NIGHTMARE ON SILENT AVE II

THE PLUG OF LIL MEXICO II

CLASSIC CITY II

By **Chris Green**

BLAST FOR ME **III**

A SAVAGE DOPEBOY III

CUTTHROAT MAFIA III

DUFFLE BAG CARTEL VII

HEARTLESS GOON VI

By **Ghost**

A HUSTLER'S DECEIT III

KILL ZONE II

BAE BELONGS TO ME III

TIL DEATH II

By **Aryanna**

KING OF THE TRAP III

By **T.J. Edwards**

GORILLAZ IN THE BAY V

3X KRAZY III

Ah'Million

STRAIGHT BEAST MODE III

De'Kari

KINGPIN KILLAZ IV

STREET KINGS III

PAID IN BLOOD III

CARTEL KILLAZ IV

DOPE GODS III

Hood Rich

SINS OF A HUSTLA II

ASAD

YAYO V

Bred In The Game 2

S. Allen

THE STREETS WILL TALK II

By Yolanda Moore

SON OF A DOPE FIEND III

HEAVEN GOT A GHETTO III

SKI MASK MONEY III

By Renta

LOYALTY AIN'T PROMISED III

By Keith Williams

I'M NOTHING WITHOUT HIS LOVE II

SINS OF A THUG II

TO THE THUG I LOVED BEFORE II

IN A HUSTLER I TRUST II

By Monet Dragun

QUIET MONEY IV

EXTENDED CLIP III

THUG LIFE IV

By **Trai'Quan**

178

THE STREETS MADE ME IV

By **Larry D. Wright**

IF YOU CROSS ME ONCE III

ANGEL V

By **Anthony Fields**

THE STREETS WILL NEVER CLOSE IV

By K'ajji

HARD AND RUTHLESS III

KILLA KOUNTY IV

By Khufu

MONEY GAME III

By Smoove Dolla

JACK BOYS VS DOPE BOYS IV

A GANGSTA'S QUR'AN V

COKE GIRLZ II

COKE BOYS II

LIFE OF A SAVAGE V

CHI'RAQ GANGSTAS V

SOSA GANG IV

BRONX SAVAGES II

BODYMORE KINGPINS II

BLOOD OF A GOON II

By Romell Tukes

MURDA WAS THE CASE III

Elijah R. Freeman

AN UNFORESEEN LOVE IV

BABY, I'M WINTERTIME COLD III

By **Meesha**

QUEEN OF THE ZOO III

Ah'Million

By **Black Migo**
CONFESSIONS OF A JACKBOY III
By Nicholas Lock
KING KILLA II
By Vincent "Vitto" Holloway
BETRAYAL OF A THUG III
By Fre$h
THE BIRTH OF A GANGSTER III
By Delmont Player
TREAL LOVE II
By Le'Monica Jackson
FOR THE LOVE OF BLOOD III
By Jamel Mitchell
RAN OFF ON DA PLUG II
By Paper Boi Rari
HOOD CONSIGLIERE III
By Keese
PRETTY GIRLS DO NASTY THINGS II
By Nicole Goosby
LOVE IN THE TRENCHES II
By Corey Robinson
FOREVER GANGSTA III
By Adrian Dulan
THE COCAINE PRINCESS IX
SUPER GREMLIN II
By King Rio
CRIME BOSS II
Playa Ray
LOYALTY IS EVERYTHING III
Molotti

It's Just Me and You 2

HERE TODAY GONE TOMORROW II
By Fly Rock
REAL G'S MOVE IN SILENCE II
By Von Diesel
GRIMEY WAYS IV
By Ray Vinci
SALUTE MY SAVAGERY II
By Fumiya Payne
BLOOD AND GAMES II
By King Dream

Available Now

RESTRAINING ORDER **I & II**
By **CA$H & Coffee**
LOVE KNOWS NO BOUNDARIES **I II & III**
By **Coffee**
RAISED AS A GOON I, II, III & IV
BRED BY THE SLUMS I, II, III
BLAST FOR ME I & II
ROTTEN TO THE CORE I II III
A BRONX TALE I, II, III
DUFFLE BAG CARTEL I II III IV V VI
HEARTLESS GOON I II III IV V
A SAVAGE DOPEBOY I II
DRUG LORDS I II III

Ah'Million

CUTTHROAT MAFIA I II
KING OF THE TRENCHES
By **Ghost**
LAY IT DOWN **I & II**
LAST OF A DYING BREED I II
BLOOD STAINS OF A SHOTTA I & II III
By **Jamaica**
LOYAL TO THE GAME I II III
LIFE OF SIN I, II III
By **TJ & Jelissa**
BLOODY COMMAS I & II
SKI MASK CARTEL I II & III
KING OF NEW YORK I II,III IV V
RISE TO POWER I II III
COKE KINGS I II III IV V
BORN HEARTLESS I II III IV
KING OF THE TRAP I II
By **T.J. Edwards**
IF LOVING HIM IS WRONG…I & II
LOVE ME EVEN WHEN IT HURTS I II III
By **Jelissa**
WHEN THE STREETS CLAP BACK I & II III
THE HEART OF A SAVAGE I II III IV
MONEY MAFIA I II
LOYAL TO THE SOIL I II III
By **Jibril Williams**
A DISTINGUISHED THUG STOLE MY HEART I II & III
LOVE SHOULDN'T HURT I II III IV
RENEGADE BOYS I II III IV
PAID IN KARMA I II III

SAVAGE STORMS I II III
AN UNFORESEEN LOVE I II III
BABY, I'M WINTERTIME COLD I II
By **Meesha**
A GANGSTER'S CODE I &, II III
A GANGSTER'S SYN I II III
THE SAVAGE LIFE I II III
CHAINED TO THE STREETS I II III
BLOOD ON THE MONEY I II III
A GANGSTA'S PAIN I II III
By J-Blunt
PUSH IT TO THE LIMIT
By **Bre' Hayes**
BLOOD OF A BOSS **I, II, III, IV, V**
SHADOWS OF THE GAME
TRAP BASTARD
By **Askari**
THE STREETS BLEED MURDER **I, II & III**
THE HEART OF A GANGSTA I II& III
By **Jerry Jackson**
CUM FOR ME I II III IV V VI VII VIII
An **LDP Erotica Collaboration**
BRIDE OF A HUSTLA **I II & II**
THE FETTI GIRLS **I, II& III**
CORRUPTED BY A GANGSTA I, II III, IV
BLINDED BY HIS LOVE
THE PRICE YOU PAY FOR LOVE I, II ,III
DOPE GIRL MAGIC I II III
By **Destiny Skai**
WHEN A GOOD GIRL GOES BAD

Ah'Million

By **Adrienne**
THE COST OF LOYALTY I II III
By Kweli
A GANGSTER'S REVENGE **I II III & IV**
THE BOSS MAN'S DAUGHTERS I II III IV V
A SAVAGE LOVE **I & II**
BAE BELONGS TO ME I II
A HUSTLER'S DECEIT I, II, III
WHAT BAD BITCHES DO I, II, III
SOUL OF A MONSTER I II III
KILL ZONE
A DOPE BOY'S QUEEN I II III
TIL DEATH
By **Aryanna**
A KINGPIN'S AMBITON
A KINGPIN'S AMBITION **II**
I MURDER FOR THE DOUGH
By **Ambitious**
TRUE SAVAGE I II III IV V VI VII
DOPE BOY MAGIC I, II, III
MIDNIGHT CARTEL I II III
CITY OF KINGZ I II
NIGHTMARE ON SILENT AVE
THE PLUG OF LIL MEXICO II
CLASSIC CITY
By **Chris Green**
A DOPEBOY'S PRAYER
By **Eddie "Wolf" Lee**
THE KING CARTEL **I, II & III**
By **Frank Gresham**

THESE NIGGAS AIN'T LOYAL **I, II & III**

By **Nikki Tee**

GANGSTA SHYT **I II &III**

By **CATO**

THE ULTIMATE BETRAYAL

By **Phoenix**

BOSS'N UP **I , II & III**

By **Royal Nicole**

I LOVE YOU TO DEATH

By **Destiny J**

I RIDE FOR MY HITTA

I STILL RIDE FOR MY HITTA

By **Misty Holt**

LOVE & CHASIN' PAPER

By **Qay Crockett**

TO DIE IN VAIN

SINS OF A HUSTLA

By **ASAD**

BROOKLYN HUSTLAZ

By **Boogsy Morina**

BROOKLYN ON LOCK I & II

By **Sonovia**

GANGSTA CITY

By **Teddy Duke**

A DRUG KING AND HIS DIAMOND I & II III

A DOPEMAN'S RICHES

HER MAN, MINE'S TOO I, II

CASH MONEY HO'S

THE WIFEY I USED TO BE I II

PRETTY GIRLS DO NASTY THINGS

Ah'Million

By Nicole Goosby

TRAPHOUSE KING **I II & III**

KINGPIN KILLAZ I II III

STREET KINGS I II

PAID IN BLOOD **I II**

CARTEL KILLAZ I II III

DOPE GODS I II

By **Hood Rich**

LIPSTICK KILLAH **I, II, III**

CRIME OF PASSION I II & III

FRIEND OR FOE I II III

By **Mimi**

STEADY MOBBN' **I, II, III**

THE STREETS STAINED MY SOUL I II III

By **Marcellus Allen**

WHO SHOT YA **I, II, III**

SON OF A DOPE FIEND I II

HEAVEN GOT A GHETTO I II

SKI MASK MONEY I II

Renta

GORILLAZ IN THE BAY **I II III IV**

TEARS OF A GANGSTA I II

3X KRAZY I II

STRAIGHT BEAST MODE I II

DE'KARI

TRIGGADALE I II III

MURDAROBER WAS THE CASE I II

Elijah R. Freeman

GOD BLESS THE TRAPPERS I, II, III

THESE SCANDALOUS STREETS I, II, III

FEAR MY GANGSTA I, II, III IV, V

THESE STREETS DON'T LOVE NOBODY I, II

BURY ME A G I, II, III, IV, V

A GANGSTA'S EMPIRE I, II, III, IV

THE DOPEMAN'S BODYGAURD I II

THE REALEST KILLAZ I II III

THE LAST OF THE OGS I II III

Tranay Adams

THE STREETS ARE CALLING

Duquie Wilson

MARRIED TO A BOSS I II III

By Destiny Skai & Chris Green

KINGZ OF THE GAME I II III IV V VI VII

CRIME BOSS

Playa Ray

SLAUGHTER GANG I II III

RUTHLESS HEART I II III

By Willie Slaughter

FUK SHYT

By Blakk Diamond

DON'T F#CK WITH MY HEART I II

By Linnea

ADDICTED TO THE DRAMA I II III

IN THE ARM OF HIS BOSS II

By Jamila

YAYO I II III IV

A SHOOTER'S AMBITION I II

BRED IN THE GAME

By S. Allen

TRAP GOD I II III

Ah'Million

RICH $AVAGE I II III
MONEY IN THE GRAVE I II III
By Martell Troublesome Bolden
FOREVER GANGSTA I II
GLOCKS ON SATIN SHEETS I II
By Adrian Dulan
TOE TAGZ I II III IV
LEVELS TO THIS SHYT I II
IT'S JUST ME AND YOU I II
By Ah'Million
KINGPIN DREAMS I II III
RAN OFF ON DA PLUG
By Paper Boi Rari
CONFESSIONS OF A GANGSTA I II III IV
CONFESSIONS OF A JACKBOY I II
By Nicholas Lock
I'M NOTHING WITHOUT HIS LOVE
SINS OF A THUG
TO THE THUG I LOVED BEFORE
A GANGSTA SAVED XMAS
IN A HUSTLER I TRUST
By Monet Dragun
CAUGHT UP IN THE LIFE I II III
THE STREETS NEVER LET GO I II III
By Robert Baptiste
NEW TO THE GAME I II III
MONEY, MURDER & MEMORIES I II III
By **Malik D. Rice**
LIFE OF A SAVAGE I II III IV
A GANGSTA'S QUR'AN I II III IV

It's Just Me and You 2

MURDA SEASON I II III

GANGLAND CARTEL I II III

CHI'RAQ GANGSTAS I II III IV

KILLERS ON ELM STREET I II III

JACK BOYZ N DA BRONX I II III

A DOPEBOY'S DREAM I II III

JACK BOYS VS DOPE BOYS I II III

COKE GIRLZ

COKE BOYS

SOSA GANG I II III

BRONX SAVAGES

BODYMORE KINGPINS

BLOOD OF A GOON

By Romell Tukes

LOYALTY AIN'T PROMISED I II

By Keith Williams

QUIET MONEY I II III

THUG LIFE I II III

EXTENDED CLIP I II

A GANGSTA'S PARADISE

By **Trai'Quan**

THE STREETS MADE ME I II III

By **Larry D. Wright**

THE ULTIMATE SACRIFICE I, II, III, IV, V, VI

KHADIFI

IF YOU CROSS ME ONCE I II

ANGEL I II III IV

IN THE BLINK OF AN EYE

By **Anthony Fields**

THE LIFE OF A HOOD STAR

189

Ah'Million

By Ca$h & Rashia Wilson
THE STREETS WILL NEVER CLOSE I II III
By K'ajji
CREAM I II III
THE STREETS WILL TALK
By Yolanda Moore
NIGHTMARES OF A HUSTLA I II III
BLOOD AND GAMES
By King Dream
CONCRETE KILLA I II III
VICIOUS LOYALTY I II III
By Kingpen
HARD AND RUTHLESS I II
MOB TOWN 251
THE BILLIONAIRE BENTLEYS I II III
REAL G'S MOVE IN SILENCE
By Von Diesel
GHOST MOB
Stilloan Robinson
MOB TIES I II III IV V VI
SOUL OF A HUSTLER, HEART OF A KILLER I II
GORILLAZ IN THE TRENCHES I II III
By SayNoMore
BODYMORE MURDERLAND I II III
THE BIRTH OF A GANGSTER I II
By Delmont Player
FOR THE LOVE OF A BOSS
By C. D. Blue
MOBBED UP I II III IV
THE BRICK MAN I II III IV V

THE COCAINE PRINCESS I II III IV V VI VII VIII

SUPER GREMLIN

By King Rio

KILLA KOUNTY I II III IV

By Khufu

MONEY GAME I II

By Smoove Dolla

A GANGSTA'S KARMA I II III

By FLAME

KING OF THE TRENCHES I II III

by **GHOST & TRANAY ADAMS**

QUEEN OF THE ZOO I II

By **Black Migo**

GRIMEY WAYS I II III

By Ray Vinci

XMAS WITH AN ATL SHOOTER

By Ca$h & Destiny Skai

KING KILLA

By Vincent "Vitto" Holloway

BETRAYAL OF A THUG I II

By Fre$h

THE MURDER QUEENS I II III

By Michael Gallon

TREAL LOVE

By Le'Monica Jackson

FOR THE LOVE OF BLOOD I II

By Jamel Mitchell

HOOD CONSIGLIERE I II

By Keese

PROTÉGÉ OF A LEGEND I II III

Ah'Million

LOVE IN THE TRENCHES
By Corey Robinson
BORN IN THE GRAVE I II III
By Self Made Tay
MOAN IN MY MOUTH
By XTASY
TORN BETWEEN A GANGSTER AND A GENTLEMAN
By J-BLUNT & Miss Kim
LOYALTY IS EVERYTHING I II
Molotti
HERE TODAY GONE TOMORROW
By Fly Rock
PILLOW PRINCESS
By S. Hawkins
NAÏVE TO THE STREETS
WOMEN LIE MEN LIE I II III
GIRLS FALL LIKE DOMINOS
STACK BEFORE YOU SPURLGE
FIFTY SHADES OF SNOW I II III
By A. Roy Milligan
SALUTE MY SAVAGERY
By Fumiya Payne

BOOKS BY LDP'S CEO, CA$H

TRUST IN NO MAN

TRUST IN NO MAN 2

TRUST IN NO MAN 3

BONDED BY BLOOD

SHORTY GOT A THUG

THUGS CRY

THUGS CRY 2

THUGS CRY 3

TRUST NO BITCH

TRUST NO BITCH 2

TRUST NO BITCH 3

TIL MY CASKET DROPS

RESTRAINING ORDER

RESTRAINING ORDER 2

IN LOVE WITH A CONVICT

LIFE OF A HOOD STAR

XMAS WITH AN ATL SHOOTER

Ah'Million